THE FLAME OF DESIRE

D0714722

What a mess! Sophie thought bitterly. She could not deny that Luke Vittorio attracted her in a way she had never imagined before, and had he loved her she would have been only too delighted to marry him. But as it was, her marriage was nothing but a mockery—because she had the best of reasons for knowing he was still carrying on his affair with her attractive stepmother . . .

THE FLAME
OF DESIRE

BY

CAROLE MORTIMER

MILLS & BOON LIMITED
15–16 BROOK'S MEWS
LONDON W1A 1DR

First published 1981
Australian copyright 1981
Philippine copyright 1981
This edition 1981

© Carole Mortimer 1981

ISBN 0 263 73607 5

Set in Monophoto Baskerville 10 on 11½ pt.

Made and printed in Great Britain by Richard Clay (The Chaucer Press), Ltd., Bungay, Suffolk

CHAPTER ONE

Sophie's father put down his newspaper long enough to look at her. 'If you go out this evening I do not want a repeat of yesterday,' he said sternly. 'We have guests arriving this afternoon and I wouldn't like them to witness a scene like last night's.'

Sophie pouted sulkily. 'That wasn't my fault.'

He looked sceptical. 'And just whose fault would you say it was? Mine? Your stepmother's? We weren't the ones trying to creep into the house at two o'clock in the morning.'

Sophie gave up all pretence of trying to look as if she were eating her breakfast. 'I'd been to a party, you knew I was going to it.'

Her stepmother pursed her lips. 'But not the time of morning you'd be arriving home. Really, Simon, this roaming about the countryside at all hours of the day and night will have to stop. After all, Sophie is only nineteen.'

Simon Bedford sighed, beginning to wish now that he hadn't brought the subject up. 'I know, Rosemary, I know, and I've already made my opinion concerning Sophie's actions last night very clear. And I trust her to see that it doesn't happen again.'

'I should hope so,' sniffed her stepmother. 'Why on earth she has to mix with those—those ruffians, I have no idea. Goodness knows we've tried to introduce her to the right sort of people.'

'Oh yes,' Sophie's mouth turned back in a sneer. 'People like Nicholas Sedgwick-Jones. He's about as exciting as a cold rice pudding!'

Her mother's eyes snapped angrily, china blue eyes set in a beautiful doll-like face. Rosemary Bedford was small and delicately made, her appearance belied by the streak of ruthlessness predominant in her personality. At thirty-six she looked much younger than her years, often being mistaken for Sophie's older sister instead of her step-mother. She had married Simon Bedford when only eight-een to his already thirty-seven, and she had exploited his love for her to the full, until now, eighteen years later, that love had turned to amused tolerance. Simon had soon come to realise that his main attraction to his young wife had been the money he possessed in abundance. And he had also realised that he couldn't hope to compete with the younger men his wife amused herself with from time to time, and had soon even given up trying to do so.

Their marriage might not be the idealistic thing he had expected it to be when they first married, but at least he had Sophie from his first marriage. Of course he and Rosemary had expected to have children of their own, he desperately wanted a son to carry on the family name and fortune, but year after year had passed with no sign of the desired child, and now they had given up hope of there ever being one.

'Nicholas is a very nice young man,' Rosemary insisted. 'And he likes you.'

'The feeling isn't reciprocated,' Sophie said scathingly. 'He's boring, pompous and egotistical. He only asks me out because he's after Daddy's money. Everyone knows the Sedgwick-Jones are broke.'

'Sophie!' her stepmother's voice rose shrilly. 'Your father didn't pay for you to go to a private school so that you could come out with things like "as exciting as a cold rice pudding'', and ''broke''. You've been taught how to talk properly, please do so.'

'Oh, Mummy, you know I'm right about Nicholas. All he can talk about is his boring old farm.'

Rosemary gave her stepdaughter a cool look. 'I'm sure his conversation is preferable to anything those hooligans you call friends have to say. Their main topics of conversation seem to be fashion and sex—and not always in that order,' her nose wrinkled her distaste. 'And look at you— you even look like them!'

Sophie was aware that her stepmother didn't approve of her long blonde hair being worn loose, or her choice of denims and tight sweaters as suitable clothing. And she didn't approve of the friends Sophie had made at the local college either, but she refused to give them up, no matter what the pressures might be.

She shrugged. 'Everyone looks like this at college.'

'Exactly! You should make an effort to remember who you are. Just think of your father's humiliation when he sees the people you go about with.' Rosemary sighed. 'Well, at least make sure you behave yourself in front of our weekend guests. A lot of them won't understand your need to rebel in this way.'

'Who's coming?' asked Sophie.

'Just a few friends, about a dozen or so.' Rosemary studied her painted nails. 'Luke Vittorio has agreed to come down.'

Simon gave her a sharp look. 'I didn't know that.'

His wife smiled at him brightly. 'I thought I'd told you, darling. He's bringing that girl he's going about with at the moment.'

'Eve Jeffers,' Sophie supplied. 'She's one of the leading models in the world at the moment.' And Luke Vittorio had been *the* fashionable portrait painter for the last ten years. He was an outrageous extrovert, his exploits almost as well known as his portraits—and his scandals. He was ruggedly attractive, emitting a sensual aura that seemed to act like a magnet on all women. And the women he attracted weren't always single.

'I know who she is, Sophie,' her stepmother snapped. 'They've been seen everywhere together the last few months.'

'I didn't know if Daddy knew her,' Sophie said defensively.

Rosemary's mouth turned back. 'I would doubt it, fashion isn't your father's strongest point—or yours either, for that matter. Look at your clothes—if those denims were any tighter they'd be indecent!'

'She's slender enough to carry them off,' Simon remarked from the depths of his newspaper. 'I couldn't give a damn what she wears as long as she's well covered. When did you invite Luke Vittorio down here?' he demanded of his wife.

'I can't remember now,' she answered vaguely. 'At Pamela's party last week, I think. What difference does it make when I invited him? He's coming, that's all we need to know.'

Simon scowled. 'I can't understand why a man like him would want to come here,' he muttered. 'He'll probably be bored within a few hours. He's used to much more exciting entertainment than we can offer.'

'Exactly,' Rosemary's mouth tightened. 'He enjoys peace and quiet like the rest of us.'

'I haven't noticed you've been enjoying it much lately. You're spending more and more time in town. I suppose the only reason we're honoured with your company this weekend is because you have all your friends coming down.'

'Don't make a scene, Simon,' his wife said impatiently.

'We've been through this so many times. I like the London society, you don't.'

'That's right, I don't. I do like to see my wife occasionally, though.'

Sophie stood up, excusing herself before this developed into a full-scale argument. There had been a lot of these arguments of late and she had found it was better to make herself scarce when one was brewing.

'Where are you going?' her stepmother demanded.

'Down to the village.'

'To see those friends of yours, I suppose?'

'To see Helen, yes.' She wouldn't be drawn into her stepmother's spiteful mood.

'I don't want you to be late back. Luke will want to have a look at you.'

'At me?' Sophie looked at her curiously. 'Whatever for?'

'Your father has commissioned him to paint you.'

She looked at her father, her eyes wide. 'Daddy?'

He was still intent on his wife. 'You asked him, Rosemary?'

'One doesn't ask Luke. He decides who he'll paint and who he won't. I merely asked him if he would look at Sophie. He'll make the final decision.'

'Daddy?' Sophie cut in, frowning her puzzlement. 'Luke Vittorio is going to paint *me*?'

'Well, he is the best, chicken. And we would like a portrait of you for the family record. It's to be your mother's birthday present to me.'

'A Luke Vittorio portrait? He'll never paint me, Daddy,' she denied. 'He only paints beautiful women. He's very exclusive. He's turned down some really important people merely because he didn't think them beautiful.'

'You're attractive enough when you take the trouble to dress properly,' her stepmother admitted grudgingly. 'And he hasn't agreed to do it yet, only to look at you.'

Sophie squirmed. 'I'm not sure I care to be "looked over" by him!'

She had seen him on a chat show on television once, a tall arrogant man who hadn't lived his thirty-eight years without being aware of his blatant good looks and cashing in on them. And he had the most piercing brown eyes she had ever seen, eyes that appeared to miss nothing, and she felt sure they didn't. He was an artist, trained to observe and take note.

He had made Sophie feel nervous just looking at him, his self-confidence awe-inspiring. And he was very mocking, making her feel quite sorry for the interviewer by the end of the programme. For someone who was so much in the public eye he was curiously clam-like about his real private life, refusing point blank to discuss any of the women in his life, except to acknowledge that there had been quite a few.

But she hadn't needed him to tell her that, she had only to open a daily newspaper to see that taunting arrogant face peering back at her, and always with a beautiful companion, and hardly ever the same one twice. He always seemed to be either entering or leaving the country, never in one place for long at a time.

'You'll do as your father and I want,' Rosemary said irritably. 'If Luke decides to paint you you'll sit for him. You can't refuse when it's to be a present to your father.'

'But his birthday isn't for months yet!'

'Three months away. And Luke can't paint you overnight. He may not even be able to start right away, in fact I'm sure he won't be able to. You have to understand that Luke isn't just any artist, he's the best of his time, able to dictate his own terms. And you'll treat him with the respect he deserves when you meet him at dinner,' she warned.

Sophie couldn't see anyone treating him any other way, he would soon put them in their place if they did. She could imagine him being quite cruel on occasion; that quirk to his mouth indicated a hardness that was a natural part of the man himself and not something he had acquired.

'What time is he arriving?' She intended making sure she wasn't here, despite her stepmother's warning. Her father was a rich and important man himself, and she didn't care to be looked over by anyone.

Her stepmother shrugged. 'When he feels like it, I would imagine. Luke lives by his own rules.'

Sophie opened the dining-room door. 'Arrogant devil!' she muttered.

'We'll have none of that when he gets here,' Rosemary said sharply.

'I'll be on my best behaviour,' Sophie promised with a certain amount of sarcasm.

'That isn't always good enough. The times you've embarrassed your father and me——'

'Let the girl go,' Simon interrupted. 'You'll only make her more determined to do the opposite of what you say.'

Sophie grinned at her father. How well he knew her! 'Thank you, Daddy.'

Her stepmother's mouth was a thin angry line. 'Why do you always side with her, Simon?' she asked petulantly, the easy tears appearing in her china-blue eyes. 'The two of you always gang up on me. It's no wonder I spend more and more time in London. I might just as well not bother to come home at all!'

Simon put his newspaper down with a sigh, realising he was in for one of the scenes that always left him feeling drained. Rosemary should never have had to cope with a child, her jealousy and spitefulness towards his only child always making it difficult for him to show any love and understanding for Sophie without a near-hysterical outburst from his wife.

'Leave us, Sophie,' he advised, standing up to put his arm about his wife. 'Now calm down, Rosemary,' he said gently. 'You're ruining your make-up.'

Sophie quietly left the room. Poor Daddy, he was in for a difficult time of it. She wondered what her stepmother would wheedle out of him this time. One of these scenes usually resulted in Rosemary acquiring something blatantly extravagant. The last time it had been a diamond brooch, the diamond being one of the biggest in the world.

She met Mrs Joyce, the housekeeper, in the hallway, a fresh pot of coffee in her hand. 'I shouldn't go in there right now,' Sophie stopped her. 'Mummy—Mummy's a little upset.'

Mrs Joyce tutted. A member of the household since Sophie had been a baby, she was as familiar with these scenes as Sophie. 'What happened this time?'

'I'm afraid it was my fault, Joycy,' Sophie used the family name for the housekeeper. 'Mummy gets upset by my behaviour. I don't mean to upset her, but I——' she broke off as her stepmother left the dining-room, no evidence of tears on her face now as she smiled at them.

'Mr Bedford's coffee, Joycy,' she smiled. 'He's never human until he's drunk several cups of your delicious brew.' She hummed to herself as she left them.

Joycy watched her mistress leave. 'I wonder what your poor father has promised her this time,' she remarked with amused tolerance.

'Something else she doesn't need,' Sophie said dully, aware that once again she had caused her father to be put in an awkward position. It was a terrible way to think, but things were a lot quieter around here when her stepmother stayed in London.

She and her father lived a peaceful existence here, her father travelling rarely to his firm situated twenty miles out of London, and she going to the local college. The two of them spent a lot of time together, a lot of their tastes being similar despite their age difference.

Joycy smiled. 'I'd better take this coffee in, it should help soothe your father.'

Sophie grimaced. 'I think he's going to need it,' was her parting comment.

Poor Daddy, she thought as she cycled the mile to Helen's house. He didn't ask much from life, just a loving wife and daughter and the continuous success of his prosperous firm. But she and her stepmother had never got on. Sophie had spent most of her childhood brought up by servants, and so every time she had met her stepmother the sparks started to fly.

Not that she didn't care for Rosemary—after all, she was the only mother she had ever known—but to Rosemary she was just a constant reminder of the passing of the years, a reminder Rosemary neither wanted or welcomed. What on earth her stepmother would do if she ever presented her with a grandchild she daren't think. Not that that was a possibility for years yet; she didn't even have a boy-friend.

Helen was out in the back garden sunbathing when Sophie arrived. 'You look hot.' She poured her out a long cool drink of lime from the jug on the table.

'I am.' Sophie collapsed on to the adjoining lounger.

'You didn't cycle over in this heat?'

Sophie sipped gratefully at the lime. 'It's quicker than walking.'

'But more exhausting. It's a pity you don't like driving.'

'I don't have the concentration. Did you get into trouble for being late last night?' she changed the subject.

Helen giggled, a petite girl with bubbly red hair and mischievous green eyes. 'This morning, you mean. Dad was furious! How about you?'

'About the same. Mummy turned up last night when I was out,' Sophie added pointedly.

Helen grimaced. 'The outcome of my late night was that Dad's forbidden me to go out for a week. He'll have forgotten all about it by tomorrow, but it means I won't be able to go anywhere tonight.'

'Neither will I. Mummy's invited some people down for the weekend, which means I have to stay in to dinner tonight.' Sophie sighed. 'I wouldn't mind, but she will insist on inviting Nicholas as my dinner partner.'

'Poor you,' Helen sympathised. 'Who's been invited for the weekend? Your mother usually knows the interesting people.'

'I only know two of the guests, Eve Jeffers and—and Luke Vittorio.'

Helen choked over her lime juice. '*Luke Vittorio*?'

'The one and only.'

Helen looked impressed. 'I saw him on television the other night. God, he's handsome. He has mesmerising come-to-bed eyes.'

'Yes.'

'And he's so dark. That must be his Italian blood, I suppose.'

'Possibly.'

Helen noticed her lack of enthusiasm for the first time. 'You aren't looking forward to him being there?'

That must be the understatement of the year! 'Most of Mummy's friends I can take, but him . . . Well, it's like Daddy said, what can we possibly do to entertain him? We aren't exactly surrounded by night spots.'

'I should think there must be lots of ways *he* could be entertained,' Helen said teasingly. 'I can think of a few ways myself.'

'He's bringing his own girl-friend down for that,' Sophie informed her with disgust. 'I don't suppose he can go for very long without a woman.'

Helen raised her eyebrows. 'What's he done to upset you? You don't usually take dislikes to people like this.'

'I'm not usually forced into their company,' she said with ill-humour. 'Mummy has asked the great man to paint me.'

That really startled Helen. 'A Luke Vittorio portrait . . .'

'That's what I said. Oh, he'll say no, of course, but I don't like the idea of him dissecting each little part of me before he rejects me. He's so damned arrogant!'

'I suppose so.'

'You don't sound very sure. I'll tell you what, come over tomorrow afternoon and you can meet him.'

Helen sat up, smiling eagerly. 'Really?' she asked excitedly.

'Yes, and welcome to him.'

Her friend laughed. 'Let's go and have a game of tennis, you can run off some of this steam. Stay for lunch and then go home when Mr Vittorio is safely installed in your house. Mum and Dad have gone out for the day shopping, so we have the house to ourselves.'

They played tennis for a couple of hours before going back to Helen's and making themselves a hamburger each. It was almost three o'clock in the afternoon by the time Sophie set off for home. She really couldn't delay any longer, she would have to change before meeting Luke Vittorio.

Her stepmother would be furious if she presented herself in tee-shirt and tight denims, and her hair was completely wild from her exertions on the tennis court. Her face was completely bare of make-up, her skin smooth and creamy, her lips a healthy pink, her violet eyes glowing as she enjoyed her ride back to her home.

She enjoyed the ride back much more than the ride to Helen's, freewheeling down the long hill that had taken such effort to get up before lunch. What breeze there was whipped through her long silver-blonde hair, her eyes glowing with pleasure.

She was almost on top of the car turning out of the side road before she saw it, and she felt sure the driver of the Mercedes hadn't seen her at all. The car was turning in from the right and she swerved precariously to avoid it, crashing up the grass verge to land in an undignified heap in a newly ploughed field.

The ground was soft to land on, but nevertheless Sophie felt shaken by the fall, peering over the tiny hedgerow at her bicycle, the wheels still spinning noisily. She sat up, rubbing her elbows which seemed to have taken the main pressure of her fall.

She looked up as a shadow fell across her, unaware of the dusty marks on her now pale cheeks, and her eyes widened with shock as she recognised the driver of the car she had swerved to avoid. Luke Vittorio!

There could be no mistaking that muscular physique clothed in fitted black silk shirt and thigh-hugging black trousers, the forbidding mouth with the full sensuous bottom lip, the hawk-like nose, the magnetic brown eyes, and the dark overlong-styled hair. He was much taller than she had imagined, well over six feet, and his skin was naturally dark instead of tanned, but there could be no doubt that this was indeed Luke Vittorio.

Sophie scrambled to her feet, hurriedly brushing down her denims so that she didn't have to look into that dark, compelling face.

'You are unhurt?' His voice was deep and husky, deeply accented despite his having lived in England and America for the last twenty years.

'Only a little bruised,' she muttered, her head bent as she studiously brushed off every bit of dust on her denims.

Nothing had prepared her for the flesh-and-blood sensuality of this man, the blatant sexuality that must surely affect every woman he came into contact with, the deep husky voice that had sexy intonations. There was something wholly primitive about the man, something untamed and untameable, and he had shaken her more than falling off her bicycle had done.

One long sensitive hand came out to grasp her forearm, his shirt sleeves turned back to just below his elbows to reveal the dark hairs against his swarthy skin, made to look even darker by the broad gold wrist-watch on his arm. Sophie couldn't take her eyes off his hand, a long tapered hand with thin sensitive fingers, an artist's hand.

'You are sure you are unharmed?' he persisted.

Sophie looked up to meet the blaze of his mesmerising brown eyes head on, deep brown eyes with a lighter brown circle around the iris. 'I'm fine,' she said breathlessly. 'I just didn't see you until it was too late.'

The hand dropped away from her arm. 'I am well aware of that.' His voice was curt, losing its silky quality. 'You were completely out of control as you came down that hill. I am only surprised there was not more damage done than there was.'

His censure angered Sophie, all the more so because she knew he was right. 'To me or to your car?' she asked sarcastically, her head thrown back, her hair streaming down her back.

'Both,' he answered abruptly. 'Is your bicycle still workable?'

She picked it up, noticing the slightly bent handlebars but determined not to tell this arrogant man. 'It seems all right to me,' she told him moodily.

He nodded impatiently. 'Would you like me to drive you anywhere?'

Sophie frowned. 'What for?'

Luke Vittorio sighed. 'I did not know if you felt too shaken to cycle the rest of the way to your home. You live on one of the hillside farms, perhaps?'

She almost laughed at his wrong assessment of her. He obviously considered her to be a simple farm girl, the thought of her being the daughter of Simon and Rosemary Bedford not even crossing his mind. It wasn't surprising considering her clothes and the fact that she was riding a dilapidated bicycle, nevertheless she found his condescension annoying, determined not to tell him of her identity and surprise him at dinner this evening. She would love to see this man squirm, and perhaps this incident had given her the ammunition to do just that.

'I live not far from here,' she evaded. 'I can make it there all right.'

'Perhaps you had better give me your address anyway.'

She raised her eyebrows. 'Why?'

'You may suffer some delayed injury. I will of course check up on your health.'

Sophie smiled, a taunting smile that held little humour. 'If I suffer any delayed injury you can be sure I'll let you know, Mr Vittorio.'

His brown eyes narrowed speculatively, sweeping over her slender figure, violet eyes and long silver-blonde hair with slow insolence. 'You know who I am?'

She gave a short laugh. 'It would be hard not to. You're a celebrity.'

He appeared unimpressed by her attempt at breathless adoration. 'Nevertheless, I think it would be better if I knew where you live.'

'There's really no need.' She concentrated on checking her cycle over, her hair falling forward in a straight gleaming curtain. 'There's really nothing wrong with me.'

'Perhaps,' he agreed. 'Your hair, is it natural?'

Her head shot up at the unexpectedness of his question.

'Well, it isn't dyed, if that's what you mean,' she said resentfully.

'And violet eyes,' he mused.

She was surprised he had noticed her hair, let alone the colour of her eyes. The artist in him again, she supposed. 'They're natural too, I'm afraid,' she answered tauntingly.

'I did not presume they were not.'

'But you doubt the naturalness of my hair.'

He shrugged his broad shoulders. 'I was merely curious.'

Sophie's attention was caught by the girl stepping elegantly out of the passenger side of the Mercedes, a girl who was instantly recognisable as Eve Jeffers. This girl was so beautiful, her features so perfect, her hair a black shining cap, her figure faultless, that she almost didn't look real.

She came to stand next to Luke Vittorio, her lacquered nails resting intimately in the crook of his arm. 'It's getting late, Luke darling,' she purred in a voice that grated on Sophie's nerve-endings. 'We should be on our way.'

Sophie bristled angrily. No concern for her health here, not even a polite query. This girl might be beautiful, but there was something about her that Sophie didn't like; perhaps it was the coldness in her eyes or the faint hardness to her mouth, but whatever it was she didn't like her.

Luke Vittorio nodded. 'You go back to the car, I will be with you in a moment.'

'We wouldn't want to keep our beautiful hostess waiting.' Eve arched an eyebrow at him. 'I'm sure she's just longing for you to arrive.'

Luke's mouth tightened. 'Go back to the car, Eve. I want no more of your innuendoes today,' he added harshly.

'I'm sure Rosemary wouldn't consider them innuendoes,' she purred. 'And then there's that brat of hers to look at,' she taunted before walking gracefully back to the car.

Sophie's anger had been increasing by the second. What

did this girl mean by these remarks about her stepmother? Of course Rosemary was looking forward to her weekend guests' arrival, but why should the model imply that she was especially looking forward to Luke Vittorio being there? She didn't like the implication behind that at all—or the implication that *she* was a brat.

He turned back to her. 'So you will not tell me where you live?'

'There's no need.' He would know soon enough! And so would Eve Jeffers, although she felt sure the other girl wouldn't give a damn.

'Very well,' he nodded curtly, before turning and walking away.

Sophie watched the car speed out of sight before making some attempt to straighten the handlebars on her bicycle. They wouldn't straighten up completely, but at least it was rideable now. She would get Martin to have a look at it when she reached home.

The Mercedes was parked alongside several other cars in the driveway as she pedalled round to the back of the house to enter through the kitchen. Her stepmother would never forgive her if she let any of the guests see her like this.

Joycy was arranging the tea things as she came into the room, but stopped what she was doing to stare at Sophie. 'What happened to you?'

She put a selfconscious hand up to her hair. 'Nothing. Why?'

'Your face is covered in dirt. What have you been doing?'

'I had a slight accident on my bicycle,' Sophie admitted sheepishly.

'Again?' Joycy shook her head. 'I've told you so many times not to use that contraption. It wobbles terribly and the brakes don't work properly.'

Sophie knew that, now. If the brakes had been working

properly she wouldn't have come off the damn thing. 'Perhaps Martin could take a look at it for me.' Martin was Joycy's husband, and her father's chauffeur and butler.

Joycy laughed. 'If I remember correctly the last time he looked at it he told you it was ready for the scrap heap.'

'But I have to have transport of some kind.'

'Martin *is* the chauffeur.'

'Transport of my own,' Sophie said patiently. 'While you take the tea things into the lounge I think I'll try and sneak up to my room.' She ran one of her dusty hands down her denims. 'I'm not really presentable.'

'You certainly aren't! You didn't hurt yourself, did you?'

'Only dented my pride a little. Flying over the handle-bars of a bike isn't exactly the height of elegance.'

Joycy frowned. 'Are you sure you're all right? You look a little pale.'

Sophie grinned. 'Well, I wouldn't mind one or two of your delicious scones to tide me over until dinner.'

'There can't be much wrong with you if you still have your appetite.' Joycy picked up the tray in preparation to leaving. 'You know where they are.'

Sophie took two of the still warm scones out of the tin, buttering them hurriedly before making her way to her room. She was going to look her very best tonight, show Luke Vittorio exactly what he would be turning down when he refused to paint her. She would show him that it wasn't only women like Eve Jeffers and her stepmother who could look beautiful. She could look quite attractive herself if she really tried, and tonight she intended trying.

She washed her hair first, drying it before she took a long leisurely bath. She came out of the bathroom smelling deliciously of pine bath-oil, the delicate perfume absorbed into her skin. The next thing to do was curl and style her hair, the natural staightness of it soon taking on a more attractive wave, two wings of hair pulled back at her temples from the centre parting to be secured loosely by two gold slides. The simplicity of the style emphasised her high cheekbones, enlarging her wide violet eyes.

She wasn't the sort of girl who usually bothered with all the feminine foibles, spending most of her life as a tomboy, but today she was making a special effort. She manicured and painted her nails a light peach colour before applying a light powdering of make-up, the lip gloss she wore exactly matching the nail varnish and the dress she had decided to wear. Her eyelashes were naturally long and dark, but she applied a light dusting of brown eye-shadow to add depth.

The peach dress was one her stepmother had taken her out and bought for her on one of her rare visits up to see her in town. Rosemary had indulged her for once, preening visibly as the saleswoman assumed them to be sisters.

The gown was Grecian in style, with a wide band of silver brocade surrounding her narrow waist. The light tan she had acquired during the last couple of months was shown to advantage against the peach chiffon, a thin delicate gold chain about her throat the only jewellery she wore.

What her stepmother and father would make of this transition she could only guess, but for all her natural poise and confidence it took great effort to go down to dinner that evening.

She smiled politely at several of the people she recognised who were gathered in the lounge, accepting the sherry Martin handed her with a broad wink in his direction. He frowned at her levity before turning away. Dear Martin, how she loved to tease him!

Luke Vittorio was already deeply engrossed in conversation with a group of people on the other side of the room, although perhaps that wasn't quite the right description. There was a tolerant smile on his dark face, but Sophie felt sure he regarded the woman talking to him with amused contempt. It was there in his eyes, in his very stance, and Sophie felt sorry for the woman as she obviously tried to make an impression on him.

He looked even more attractive than he had this afternoon, the blue velvet jacket fitting tautly across his wide powerful shoulders, the white shirt flamboyantly frilled at the front although not effeminately so. He wore black trousers, his legs long and muscular beneath the fitted material.

'So we meet again after all.'

She turned sharply at the sound of that huskily accented voice, the man she had been talking to drifting off as he knew himself overshadowed by the other man. As she had been standing with her back towards him she had no idea how Luke Vittorio had known it was her.

She gave him a cool nod. 'Mr Vittorio.'

'Please, call me Luke,' he invited smoothly. 'And I may call you——?'

'You may call me——'

'Ah, Luke,' her stepmother came over to them, extra-ordinarily beautiful in the flowing red figure-hugging gown. 'I see you've met my little Sophie.'

Sophie cringed, feeling about five years old. But then her stepmother would probably have preferred it if she were, much less ageing to herself. She looked up into the narrowed brown eyes of Luke Vittorio with defiance. 'Mr Vittorio and I haven't yet introduced ourselves, Mummy,' and she gave him a challenging smile.

CHAPTER TWO

SHE had felt sure he was taken aback by her identity, but there was no evidence of it now in his chillingly handsome face. 'This is your daughter, Rosemary?' he queried softly.

Her stepmother gave a brittle laugh. 'This is my step-daughter, yes.'

Those deep brown eyes were levelled on Sophie again. 'I did not realise.'

'Do introduce yourself properly, Sophie,' Rosemary gave her an angry glare. 'I have to go and save your father from Monty again. He will insist on talking for hours about horse-racing,' she explained to Luke, 'and Simon has no interest in it at all.'

'You did not think it necessary to introduce yourself this afternoon?' Luke Vittorio asked abruptly once her stepmother had left them in a haze of her cloying perfume.

Sophie placed her empty sherry glass down on the side-table with relaxed calm. 'Should I have done?'

'I would have thought it polite, considering you know my reason for being here.'

She arched her eyebrows. 'Do I?'

'I would have thought so,' he said coolly.

Her mouth twisted as she remembered the way her step-mother had said this man was going to 'look her over'. 'I'm not exactly what you expected, am I?' she challenged.

His head was held at a haughty angle, his eyes narrowed. 'And what did I expect?'

'I believe Miss Jeffers described it as a—brat?'

'I am not Miss Jeffers.' His voice was distinctly cool now.

Sophie gave a light laugh. 'I'm aware of that. But I believe you expected someone a little—younger?'

He nodded distantly, the black sheen of his hair catching the overhead light. 'Perhaps.'

There was no perhaps about it. She had known as soon as Eve Jeffers had called her a brat that they were expecting a much younger girl, possibly someone of ten or eleven. 'And what do you think now?'

He shrugged his broad shoulders, muscle rippling beneath his velvet jacket. 'Your age is irrelevant as to whether I paint you or not. As a matter of interest, how old are you?'

'I'm not sure my stepmother would want me to tell you that. She's just old enough to be my real mother.'

He gave a mocking smile. 'I am sure you are right when you say Rosemary would not like me to know that—she has a way of looking constantly young.' His admiring eyes followed her stepmother as she flitted about the room talking to her guests.

'And a stepdaughter of nineteen isn't very flattering,' Sophie said abruptly, not liking the way he was looking at Rosemary. It brought back the feeling of uneasiness she had felt at Eve Jeffers' disparaging remarks about Rosemary this afternoon.

Luke Vittorio smiled fully now, showing his firm even white teeth. 'I am sure Rosemary would not think so.'

Sophie's resentment grew, but she was prevented from making any reply by the arrival of Eve Jeffers at Luke Vittorio's side, the pebble-green eyes flicking over her speculatively. That brief glance was enough to show Sophie that she wasn't considered a rival.

'Sorry I'm late down, Luke darling,' Eve said throatily, her hand in the crook of his arm. 'I haven't missed anything, have I?' she asked maliciously.

Sophie revised her earlier opinion of this woman being beautiful; there was too much hardness about her and a cruel twist to her painted lips for her to merit such a description. Not that she didn't look pure perfection in the green gypsy-style evening dress, there was just a hardness about her that marred that beauty.

'You have missed being introduced to Miss Bedford,' he informed her.

The black eyebrows arched. 'The brat?' She looked around. 'Has she been sent to bed already? Oh well, spoilt kids aren't amongst my favourite people anyway.' She looked back at Sophie. 'Do I know you?'

'No,' Sophie said stiffly.

Eve frowned. 'I've seen you before, I'm sure of it. Are you a model too?'

'You flatter me!'

'Sophie!' She looked up as she heard her name called, seeing Nicholas Sedgwick-Jones making his way towards her. She groaned inwardly as he beamed down at her, waiting for his opening line as she always did. 'You're looking particularly beautiful tonight,' he gushed.

This time she did groan. Nicholas always said the same thing, it was only the time of day that changed. It wouldn't have been so bad if she didn't suspect his widowed mother of teaching it to him parrot-fashion before he came out every day; there was certainly no sincerity behind his words.

She made the introductions to the other couple, aware that Luke Vittorio regarded Nicholas with as much contempt as she did. Luckily they all started going in to dinner at that moment, although she didn't think herself so lucky a few seconds later when Luke Vittorio offered her his arm to go in to dinner.

She had no choice but to accept. 'Shouldn't you be

taking in your girl-friend?' she said tartly once out of ear-shot of the other two.

'I am sure Eve will be suitably entertained by your friend.'

As she could already hear Nicholas launching into an account of his life on his farm Sophie didn't feel sure of any such thing. Nicholas bored her, so what he would do to the much more sophisticated model she had no idea. He was still enthusing about his favourite subject as they came into the dining-room, and Sophie felt almost sorry for the other girl as she saw her mother had placed them next to each other at dinner.

She didn't feel so elated when she found herself seated next to Luke Vittorio. Her mother sat at the head of the table, Luke sitting to her left and Sophie next to him. Nicholas and Eve were sitting at the other end of the table.

'Has Sophie managed to introduce herself yet?' Rosemary asked Luke.

'Oh yes,' he nodded.

'I think Mr Vittorio was under a mishapprehension, Mummy,' Sophie said with relish, forking melon into her mouth.

'About what, Sophie?' her stepmother frowned.

'About the age of your stepdaughter, Rosemary,' Luke cut in. 'I believed someone as beautiful as yourself could not possibly be the mother of a nineteen-year-old girl. Your stepdaughter seems to find my error amusing.'

'Sophie is a naughty child.' Rosemary put her hand intimately on his arm. 'I hope you'll consider her worthy of your talent.'

And Sophie hoped he wouldn't! She had had enough of his arrogance already, let alone having to sit for him for possibly hours on end. 'I'm sure Mr Vittorio is much too busy to paint me,' she protested.

His dark eyes mocked her. 'I have not yet made up my mind.'

She bristled angrily. 'Well, I have,' she said crossly. 'I don't want to be painted, by you or anyone else.'

'Sophie!' there was an angry flush to her stepmother's smooth creamy skin. 'You'll do as you're told.'

'I do not paint unwilling subjects,' Luke Vittorio stated haughtily.

Sophie felt sure that all the women he painted were more than willing, and not just to have their portrait painted. 'Good,' she smiled happily. 'That lets me out.'

'Sophie!' once again Rosemary gasped.

'I'm sure Mr Vittorio understands,' Sophie said uncaringly.

'And I'm just as sure he doesn't,' her stepmother's voice was harsh. 'I'm so sorry, Luke,' she gave him a glowing smile, 'Sophie isn't normally this rude.'

Only to people as arrogant and condescending as this man! 'Have I been rude?' she queried with feigned innocence.

Rosemary's mouth was set in an angry line. 'You know very well you have.'

'Then I apologise,' she said in the same offhand manner she had carried out the rest of the conversation. 'But I was only telling Mr Vittorio the way I felt.'

He gave her a cool look. 'The fact that the portrait is to be a gift to your father is of no consequence to you?'

She blushed at his intended rebuke. 'I'm sure Daddy will survive without it.'

'I believe it was to have been a birthday present, an addition to the family record.'

'And would you like that, Mr Vittorio, to be the painter of one of our family portraits?'

He shrugged his broad shoulders. 'It does not bother me

one way or the other. I paint only what I want to paint. What my client does with that painting once it has been completed is none of my concern.'

Rosemary gave a light tinkling laugh. 'Every portrait you do is highly acclaimed, Luke, and they're always kept in a place of honour.'

'I'm sure they are,' Sophie put in dryly, sipping her wine.

'If you can't be civil,' her stepmother snapped, 'then don't say anything at all!'

Sophie shrugged. 'That suits me.'

After that she devoted all her attention to the man sitting to her left, dazzling him with her laughing violet eyes, flattering him outrageously. And all the time she was aware of the soft murmuring of conversation between her step-mother and Luke Vittorio. Not that she could hear what was being said, they were talking too quietly for that.

Her stepmother was the gracious hostess to this sophisti-cated man, and yet Sophie knew that *she* would be in for a certain amount of angry reprisal once her stepmother had her alone. She had in fact been more outspoken than she intended, but she didn't regret it. Her stepmother might like the man, enjoy his company, but *she* wasn't going to become another of the women following him with adoring eyes. She didn't much like the attention Rosemary paid him either, and she could see her father watching them closely too.

Nicholas managed to be at her side again as they stood in the lounge drinking coffee. His boyish face always looked pink and well scrubbed, his fair hair kept short and brushed away from his forehead. Sophie supposed he could be called good-looking—if only he didn't have such a boring turn of conversation. He was doing it again now, launching into a lengthy tale about a sick cow he had.

'Of course I knew the diagnosis before the vet told me,' he said enthusiastically, 'but you have to call these chaps out just to confirm it.'

'Yes, of course you do,' she agreed vaguely, watching as her stepmother continued to stay at Luke Vittorio's side. He was obviously the guest of honour, a feather in Rosemary's social cap, but it really wasn't like her to neglect her other guests like this.

'I—er—I don't suppose you would care to come over to tea tomorrow?' Nicholas looked at her expectantly. 'My mother would love to see you.'

Sophie didn't doubt it. Every time she saw Mrs Sedgwick-Jones she extolled the virtues of her only child, hinting broadly at how she would welcome Sophie as a member of the family. The Sedgwick-Joneses might have breeding, but they had very little money to go with it. It wouldn't be so bad if Rosemary didn't encourage them, inviting Nicholas over here every chance she had.

She shook her head. 'I don't think I can, Nicholas, not with all these guests here. It wouldn't look very good if I just disappeared tomorrow afternoon.'

'But they aren't your guests,' he persisted. 'And I'm sure your stepmother wouldn't mind. Besides, these people aren't even in your age group.'

Neither was he, if the truth were known. He might only be twenty-three, but he acted much older. 'I don't think I should,' she refused. 'Not when we have guests.'

And one guest in particular. It was a disquieting feeling seeing her stepmother's head bent towards that dark one so often, and her feelings of unease increased as she saw the frown on her father's face.

'He's a distinguished-looking chap, isn't he?' Nicholas remarked at her side, drawing her attention back to him. 'Mm?'

'Luke Vittorio,' he explained. 'He's a very noticeable chap.'

He had obviously followed her line of vision and misunderstood her interest. 'I suppose you could say that,' she acknowledged ruefully.

'He's not what you expect of an artist, though, is he?' Sophie gave an amused smile. 'And what did you expect? The classical paint-stained smock, the paintbrush behind each ear?'

A dark hue coloured his cheeks. 'Now you're mocking me!'

She put a hand on his arm. 'Only a little,' she gave him an apologetic smile. 'But Mr Vittorio could hardly sit down to dinner in his working clothes. I'm sure he wears denims and tee-shirts when he paints.' And looked just as distinguished in them as he did his other clothes. The man carried himself with arrogant elegance and would stand out in a crowd no matter what he wore.

'You seemed to have a lot to say to him at dinner,' observed Nicholas.

'I'm surprised you noticed,' she teased. 'You seemed pretty well occupied with Eve Jeffers.' She had seen the other girl trying to stifle a couple of yawns as Nicholas didn't stop talking throughout the whole meal.

Again he blushed, although she thought he was secretly pleased about her noticing such a thing. He perhaps, mistakenly, thought her to be jealous.

'Miss Jeffers was very interested in that sick cow I was telling you about.'

She shook her head. Poor Nicholas, he had no idea how boring he was. She looked up to find a pair of deep brown eyes watching her with mocking amusement, and glared resentfully at Luke Vittorio, guessing that Nicholas was the reason for his amusement. Her stepmother seemed to have momentarily left the man's side, although he wasn't short of company, surrounded as he was by a group of the female guests.

Sophie put her hand in the crook of Nicholas' arm, leading him purposefully over to the chattering group. She edged her way in to stand at Luke Vittorio's side, giving him a dazzling smile as he looked down at her questioningly.

'Would you care for some more coffee?' she asked him politely.

He seemed surprised by her friendly attitude after her earlier rudeness, his eyes narrowing. 'No, thank you. Your stepmother has seen to my needs.'

Sophie's mouth tightened. Not all of them she hadn't! 'Nicholas has been longing to talk to you,' she pulled the shy young man forward. 'There wasn't time before dinner.'

'Oh, but——' Nicholas began to protest.

She patted his arm. 'Now don't be shy, Nicholas. I'm sure Mr Vittorio would love to hear about your farm. Tell him about that poor sick cow you had.'

Nicholas looked uncomfortable. 'I'm sure that can be of no interest——'

'Of course it would,' she encouraged, surprised that for once he seemed to have realised someone had no interest in the welfare of his animals. 'I'll just go and make sure our other guests have everything they need. I won't be long.'

'But——'

She gave a mischievous smile before walking away. She would teach Luke Vittorio to laugh at her. Let him listen to Nicholas and see how he fared!

He seemed to be faring very well ten minutes later when she looked over at him; the two men were apparently deep in conversation.

She turned away angrily, accepting a glass of champagne from the tray Martin was offering to the guests. She had quite expected Luke Vittorio to excuse himself as soon as it was polite to do so, but no, he seemed quite content to talk to Nicholas.

'The stem of that glass is not my throat,' he said from close behind her.

Sophie turned hurriedly to confront the artist, releasing the tight grip she had on the glass. 'Do you have reason to think it was?' she returned lightly.

'Oh, yes,' he gave a slight smile. 'Do you not think it was rather cruel of you to leave your young friend like that?'

Her violet eyes glowed her malicious pleasure. 'Didn't you enjoy your little chat with him?'

'I enjoyed it very much. I thought you cruel to Mr Sedgwick-Jones, not myself.'

'To Nicholas?' she frowned her puzzlement.

'Yes. I am sure he came here this evening with the sole purpose of being with you. He did not expect to have to answer my quite extensive questioning about his livestock.'

She gave him a suspicious look. 'Extensive questioning?'

He gave an inclination of his dark head. 'I have a farm myself in America—or perhaps you would call it a ranch.'

'You have a ranch?' She was aware that she was repeating everything he said, but he had taken her aback. She had fully expected him to be as bored with Nicholas as everyone else seemed to be.

'A few acres,' he confirmed.

She felt sure that 'a few acres' amounted to hundreds, possibly thousands. 'But your home is in London,' she pointed out.

'I have no—home. I live where it suits me, and no doubt one day it will suit me to live in America. I have a manager there at the moment, but I visit from time to time.'

She could just see this man astride a horse, master of all he surveyed. The healthy tinge to his swarthy skin indicated that he did not spend all of his time working indoors and socialising now. No, there was power in his muscular physique, not an ounce of superfluous flesh on his tall agile body.

'So you can understand,' he continued, 'that I found your friend's conversation very interesting. He is very knowledgeable on certain subjects.'

'Yes,' she agreed tightly.

The amusement in his dark eyes deepened. 'You did not expect me to find him so,' he mocked.

Sophie gave him a furious look. 'Are you always so arrogant and—and emotionless?' she snapped.

Luke's mockery became more pronounced. 'I do not think I am the one to ask about that. I have all the usual male appetites and emotions.'

'I know that,' she sneered. 'And not all of your conquests are single wom . . .' She broke off, looking with horror from him to her stepmother and back again. Oh no, she couldn't believe it, not Rosemary and this man! But what other explanation could there be, why else did her father look so anxious and her stepmother so glowingly beautiful?

She had always known that her stepmother and father didn't have the normal marriage of her friends' parents, the two of them enjoyed a different life-style, but that Rosemary could be interested in another man had never occurred to her. They had always appeared fond of each other, but she doubted her parents were actually *in* love with each other. But another man . . .

'You have gone very pale.' Luke Vittorio stood in front of her, shielding her from the rest of the people in the room. 'Are you feeling unwell?'

She swallowed hard, nausea rising up in her throat. 'I—I feel sick,' she choked, unable to look at him.

'I think you should go to your room and lie down,' he advised. 'Perhaps you would like me——'

'I wouldn't like *you* to do anything,' she snapped, her eyes flashing her dislike.

'Why me in particular?'

She glared at him. 'I think you know the answer to that. Excuse me, I can't bear——'

'Luke,' Eve Jeffers came up to them, smiling broadly, 'I can't seem to get you alone this evening.' She gave Sophie a disparaging look. 'The Bedford women seem to be monopolising your attention.'

At least she had progressed from a brat to a woman! And she understood this woman's reference to her stepmother looking forward to Luke's arrival now, understood it and hated it. And she hated him! He had no right to encourage her stepmother in this folly, to use his sensuality like a fly-trap against Rosemary's ever-increasing consciousness of the coming of middle age, her awareness of the passing of the years.

She gave the other girl a tight smile. 'You can have him back now,' she gave Luke a look of intense dislike. 'I've finished with him.'

'Well, really!' Eve Jeffers gasped.

Sophie didn't wait to hear any more. She wanted only to escape, to go to her room and be sick, to wallow in her own misery. She didn't need to look up as she was pulled round, knowing that her accoster must be Luke Vittorio.

'What do you want?' she demanded nastily.

'I do not care to be dismissed in that way,' he told her coldly.

Sophie didn't know how she could ever have thought his eyes magnetically seductive. Right now they were like hard angry pebbles, although she managed to meet his gaze with haughty defiance. She wouldn't be daunted by him, not by a man she hated and despised.

'Well, that's too bad,' she answered. 'Because I've certainly dismissed you. I don't like you, Mr Vittorio, and I make no secret of the fact.'

'You most certainly do not. I would be interested to know the reason for this dislike.'

She looked pointedly at her stepmother. 'I'm sure you're well aware of the reason. Let go of me!' She shook off his hand.

'You are indeed a brat.' His dark eyes swept over her scathingly.

'That's right,' there was challenge in every curve of her body. 'I should try to remember that before you go any further.'

He frowned. 'Any further in what?'

'You have your girl-friend here, let that be enough for you.'

Luke gave a short husky laugh. 'You are surely not implying that I am interested in you?' Again he laughed. 'You could not be more wrong.'

Sophie snatched her arm out of his grasp. 'I should damn well think so!' her eyes spat her hatred of him. 'I think one female member of this family under your spell is enough!'

He shook his head, his hand falling to his side. 'You surely do not suspect——'

'Suspect!' she cut in shrilly. 'I suppose that's the right word for what you and my stepmother are doing. I more than *suspect* you, Mr Vittorio, and I'm sure a lot of other people do too.' Her father included!

'You could not be more wrong.'

'I couldn't be more *right*! Oh, I'll admit that my step-mother ought to have more sense, but no doubt you can be flattering enough when you choose to be. She can't exactly be blamed for her infatuation, I'm sure you encourage her. But let me tell you this,' a hard determination entered her voice. 'If my father ever finds out, if you ever hurt him in any way I'll make you pay for it. I don't know how, but I'll find a way.'

'You love your father very much?' He appeared unperturbed by her heated threat.

She flushed at his complete disregard for what she had said. 'Of course I love my father,' she snapped.

'And your stepmother also?' he pressed quietly.

'That's a stupid question,' she said abruptly, aware that her love for her stepmother was not the spontaneous affection she felt for her father but more a love formed out of duty. And she had a feeling this man knew that!

It was something she had worried about when she was younger, but as her stepmother made it clear she preferred not to be bothered with anything maternal she had come to realise that any affection on her part would be regarded with distaste by Rosemary. It had been a painful thing to accept, but at least she could feel happy at her father's place in her stepmother's affections. At least, she had! If this man did anything to spoil that . . .

'You have not answered me,' Luke Vittorio broke into her thoughts.

She gave him a look of irritation. 'I thought I had,' she said curtly. 'Just stay away from my family, Mr Vittorio.'

His eyes deepened with mockery. 'That will not be easy. I am, after all, a guest of your family.'

'Of my stepmother,' she corrected. 'Don't expect anything but contempt from me!' She swung away from him, her room seeming even more of a haven now.

'Sophie? Sophie, where are you going?'

She inwardly groaned as she recognised Nicholas's voice. She had forgotten his very existence the last few minutes. She fixed a smile on her face before turning to face him.

'How are you enjoying yourself, Nicholas?' she asked politely.

'Well, I—It's all right, I suppose. But I came here to see you. You haven't said yet whether you'll come over for tea tomorrow.'

She was even more determined not to leave the house tomorrow now. She wanted to keep her eye on her stepmother and Luke Vittorio. 'Not tomorrow, Nicholas. Perhaps next weekend,' she added at the disappointment on his face.

'You promise?' he clutched at her hand.

'I can't promise that, Nicholas,' she answered lightly, doing her best to release her hand without appearing too obvious. 'Ask me later in the week.'

'Oh, but——'

'Please, Nicholas,' she put up a hand to her throbbing temple. 'Don't go on about it now. I—I can't think straight.'

He frowned his concern. 'Aren't you feeling well?'

She gave a strained smile. 'It's just a sick headache. I was going to lie down when you stopped me.'

'Without saying goodnight to me?'

Sophie sighed. 'I just want to lie down, Nicholas. Good manners don't come into it when you feel like this.'

'No, of course not. How thoughtless of me. I——'

'Are you all right, Sophie?' Her father had come to stand at her side. Her pale face must have answered for her. 'Come on,' he put an arm about her shoulders, 'let's get you up to your room.'

She smiled at him gratefully. 'Call me in the week, Nicholas,' she called, hoping he would do no such thing.

Her father guided her up to her room before helping her to undress and get into bed. He bathed her hot forehead for her. 'Now, what happened to you?' he asked gently. 'Too much wine?'

She grinned ruefully, knowing she could never tell him

the real reason for her sudden sickness. 'Probably,' she agreed.

'I don't suppose young Sedgwick-Jones helped,' he smoothed back her hair. 'He really is a pushy young man.'

Sophie smiled at the understatement. She looked at her father, noting how handsome he was even now at fifty-five. He was a tall man, not running to fat as many of his contemporaries were, with only faint touches of grey in his thick brown hair, a handsome, distinguished man in his own right, and yet for some reason he and her stepmother had lost that vital spark between them.

Seeing her stepmother's obvious interest in Luke Vittorio had opened her eyes to so many things. It wasn't just her parents' apparent differences in life-style that held them apart, there was something else too. She had only noticed this coldness between them the last couple of years, her stepmother's more and more frequent visits up to London. Or perhaps it had always been there and she hadn't noticed it; she had been away at boarding-school until she was seventeen and hadn't had chance to observe them together that much.

But she was sure her father was still deeply in love with Rosemary, knew that he could be deeply hurt by Luke Vittorio. But she wouldn't let it happen, would stop it somehow.

She smiled shakily at her father as he tucked the covers in around her. 'I love you, Daddy,' she said huskily.

He gave her a strange look, a slight frown on his face. 'I know you do, poppet. And I love you. Rest now, try to get some sleep. And no wine for you next time.'

Sophie kept up her smile until he had left the room. She didn't know how she was going to do it, but she was going to stop this affair between her stepmother and Luke Vittorio. After all, there couldn't be anything serious between them, certainly not on Luke Vittorio's part anyway; his affairs were well known.

And he had brought Eve Jeffers with him, although she could just be a smoke-screen. The model seemed to know something was going on, but perhaps she didn't know enough. Or perhaps she didn't care. There was no chance of the affair becoming a serious one, so perhaps the model was just biding her time. That seemed the most logical explanation, and it would explain her bitchiness towards Rosemary.

Sophie looked up with a start as her stepmother came into the room. She couldn't remember the last time Rosemary had been in here.

Her stepmother looked down at her. 'Your father tells me you aren't feeling well.'

'No,' she agreed huskily, kneading the sheet between thumb and finger.

'What's wrong with you?'

'Just a sick headache.'

Rosemary frowned. 'Your father seemed to think it was the wine.'

'Yes.'

'I suppose this is your excuse for your rudeness earlier on,' Rosemary snapped.

Sophie had known this was coming, had known since her outburst to Luke Vittorio at the dinner table that her stepmother would not let the incident pass. And in the light of her discovery about the two of them Rosemary's anger was all the more understandable. She wouldn't want to lose the handsome Italian because of the rudeness of her stepdaughter.

'Yes,' she nodded.

Her stepmother's blue eyes were coldly angry. 'What sort of an answer is that?'

'I—Well, I just don't like Mr Vittorio.' Was it her imagination or did she see a faint glimmer of relief in her stepmother's face? If she had it didn't show now.

'Don't be ridiculous, everyone likes Luke.'

'Well, I don't,' Sophie said sulkily.

'It isn't that important anyway. He'll only be painting you, nothing else.'

Oh yes, he would, he would be providing a perfectly respectable reason for her stepmother and himself to keep in contact, to occasionally be seen together. Well, not if she could help it!

'I don't want to be painted by him.'

'You'll do as you're told.' Rosemary had obviously run out of patience with her. 'And I don't want any more rudeness to him. Your father would be very shocked if he knew about your behaviour.'

Not if he knew the real reason behind it! 'Yes, Mummy.'

Rosemary gave her a sharp look, suspecting sarcasm and finding none. 'I'll see you in the morning,' and she slammed out of the room.

Sophie kept a watchful eye on her stepmother and Luke Vittorio all the next day, although there was really nothing to witness today. Perhaps Luke Vittorio had learnt by his folly of yesterday, but he seemed to keep a polite distance between himself and the other guests, Eve Jeffers being the only person he appeared to talk to.

Helen duly arrived for tea, blushing profusely after Sophie had introduced her to the artist. 'Gosh, he's lovely!' She couldn't take her eyes off him.

Sophie gave her a disgusted look. 'He's arrogant and conceited.'

Helen's eyes widened before her gaze wandered back to Luke Vittorio as he stood talking to Sophie's father on the other side of the room. She couldn't seem to see anything but the handsome Luke Vittorio, loving the way the cream trousers and shirt clung to his muscular body and accentuated his swarthy colouring.

'Surely not?' she said breathlessly.

'Believe me, he is.' And he had no right to be talking so casually to her father, not when he was having an affair with his wife. But a man like that wouldn't give a damn.

'Ooh, look!' squealed Helen. 'They're coming over!'

And they were too, the two men talking amicably together. Her poor father, it wouldn't occur to him to suspect this man of being interested in his wife.

Her father smiled at the two girls. 'Mr Vittorio—Luke, has just been telling me that he would very much like to paint you, Sophie,' he told her triumphantly.

She raised shocked eyes to that dark satanic face, flinching at the cold disdain for her in his eyes. 'I don't——'

'Of course I will not be able to travel down here for your sittings,' Luke Vittorio spoke for the first time. 'You will have to visit me at my apartment in London for that.'

CHAPTER THREE

'OH, but——'

Her father frowned. 'Surely that isn't necessary, Luke. A couple of sittings down here would be enough.'

Luke shook his head. 'I am afraid not. I do not work that way. I cannot work from sketches, and as I said, I do not have the time to travel down here for the necessary sittings.'

Sophie was speechless after her first words of protest. She didn't want to travel up to London to see this man, visit his apartment, spend any more time in his company than she needed to. The glittering satisfaction in his deep brown eyes told her that he was enjoying her discomfort, and she knew with sudden clarity that this was his revenge on her for her rudeness of yesterday. Well, his satisfaction would be short-lived.

'Mr Vittorio's right, Daddy,' she said with a smile, looking for some sign of surprise on the artist's face and finding none. An expert at hiding his true feelings, was this man. That just made her all the more determined to thwart him. If he expected her to protest at his proposed plan he was going to be disappointed. 'I can travel up to London at the weekends. I could stay at the apartment with Mummy,' and so make it awkward for the couple to meet!

Her father looked undecided. 'I suppose it is a solution. I must admit that when your mother first suggested this I didn't realise I would have to lose my daughter's company at the weekends too.'

'Perhaps Mummy will come home and keep you company.' Although she doubted it, she doubted it very much.

As if on cue her stepmother joined their little group, smiling her pleasure when told of the proposed portrait. She put her hand in the crook of Luke's arm, smiling up at him, looking very petite against his superior height. 'That's marvellous, Luke,' she said huskily. 'It means we'll see a little more of you.'

Not if Sophie could help it! Perhaps this was a good idea after all, perhaps this was a way to stop this affair before it became too important. 'Not really, Mummy,' she put in quietly. 'It just means *I'll* see more of Mr Vittorio.'

China-blue eyes narrowed. 'What do you mean?' The seductive purr was gone from her voice.

'I'll be staying at the apartment and visiting Mr Vittorio at his home.' The way she put it it sounded like an intimate arrangement.

A fact Luke Vittorio was quick to notice. 'For professional reasons only,' he said softly.

'But of course,' she glared at him. The remark hadn't been meant for him.

'Yes, of course,' her stepmother echoed sharply. 'And when is all this to start?'

'I will call Sophie when I am free,' Luke replied. 'It will not be for a few weeks yet, I am engaged in other work at the moment.'

Sophie didn't speak to him again until after dinner, but deliberately sought him out before he left. 'I'll look forward to seeing you again, Mr Vittorio,' she said tauntingly.

'I am sure you will,' he returned mockingly.

'Just tell me this, why did you agree to paint me?' Her curiosity had got the better of her.

He raised a dark eyebrow as he slowly studied her from head to foot. 'Why should I not? You will make an interesting study. There is a coolness outside belied by the heated passion inside. I will enjoy trying to capture this elusiveness of yours.'

Sophie's face was fiery red by this time. 'I'm sure you're reading things into my character that simply aren't there.'

'I do not think so.' He crossed one well-shod foot over the other.

They were seated together on one of the sofas, Sophie slightly unnerved by his closeness. He was clothed in a cream suit and brown shirt open at the neck to reveal the start of the thick mat of hair that she felt sure covered most of his body, and if anything he looked even more attractive than he had the previous evening. He would be leaving shortly which probably accounted for his less formal attire.

'I do,' she disagreed. 'It isn't heated passion you can detect, it's burning anger.'

'We shall see.'

'*We* most certainly will not!' She sat forward in her agitation.

Luke laughted softly. 'How you delight in jumping to conclusions! You seem to do it often where I am concerned. One of these days you will realise how foolish your thoughts are concerning myself.' He stood up. 'But not yet. That will come with time.'

'Time is something I don't intend to give you too much of,' she glared up at him.

'You will give me all the time I want,' he told her haughtily. 'It could lead to some awkward questions from your father if you do not—and I am sure you would not want that. Would you?'

'No, I wouldn't, damn you! Is this portrait so important to you that you'll go to these lengths?' she demanded disgustedly.

He shrugged. 'I will not know that until I actually begin. I look forward to seeing you again soon,' he bowed arrogantly.

'I'll make sure it's a memorable meeting!'

His teeth flashed whitely in his swarthy face. 'I am sure you will.'

Sophie didn't feel quite so confident as she travelled up to London for her first sitting four weeks later. She wasn't looking forward to seeing him again, for all her bravado at their last meeting. As it had turned out she hadn't been the one to talk to him on the telephone when he finally rang to arrange this sitting, she had been at Nicholas's, having at last given in to his persuadings to visit his house for tea.

As she had expected, Mrs Sedgwick-Jones hadn't

stopped listing her son's virtues all the time she was there, virtues that to Sophie seemed to make him even more unsuitable as a husband for her. She was disappointed therefore when she returned home to find Luke Vittorio had telephoned in her absence, disappointed because she would have enjoyed another of their verbal clashes.

But now she was going to London and would see him face to face, and she found the prospect a little daunting. Today she would be meeting him on his home ground, and she was very aware of the fact that she would be at a disadvantage. As a guest in her parents' home he had not been as forthright as she suspected he could have been, but any rudeness from her here would not go unpunished.

But first she had to face her stepmother. The two of them had seen little of each other the last four weeks and Sophie could feel herself tensing for their meeting as she travelled in the taxi from the station.

As it turned out she needn't have worried; Rosemary was out when she reached the apartment, and a solitary lunch was served to her by Bernard the butler. He was a silent individual, revealing only that her stepmother had gone shopping and was meeting friends for lunch. She hadn't expected Rosemany to be overjoyed to see her, but she hadn't expected her to be out altogether either.

She had no idea what she was supposed to wear for this painting; Luke Vittorio hadn't said and she hadn't thought to ask. Her stepmother could probably have advised her, but she hadn't been very approachable lately, in fact she had rarely been home. Consequently Sophie had brought a couple of dresses with her, hoping to consult her stepmother when she reached London. She had travelled down in denims and a purple sun-top, having decided to have a refreshing shower before changing for her meeting with Luke Vittorio.

Her stepmother came into her bedroom just as she was

coming out of the bathroom, her hair secured on top of her head, her only cover a luxurious bathtowel. She looked uncertainly at Rosemary, not sure of her welcome.

'So you've arrived,' her stepmother snapped.

So she had been right to feel unsure; her stepmother definitely wasn't pleased to see her. 'Yes,' she answered quietly, unpacking fresh underwear so that Rosemany shouldn't see her nervousness.

Rosemary was looking beautiful in an emerald-coloured silk dress that clung to her curves before flaring out from her narrow waist, her shoulder-length hair curled provocatively about her beautiful face. She picked up the denims and sun-top with obvious distaste. 'You surely aren't thinking of wearing these?'

'Well, I——'

'God, how you love to disgrace your father and me! Didn't you bring anything more suitable to wear? I'm sure Luke didn't intend for you to look like a street urchin.'

'I couldn't give a damn what *Luke* wants me to look like.'

Her stepmother's eyebrows rose tauntingly. 'Of course, you don't like Luke, do you?'

'I can't stand the man!'

'Perhaps that's as well,' Rosemary said throatily. 'I'm sure he wouldn't care to be bothered with a teenage crush.'

Sophie gave a hard laugh. 'He has no need to fear that.'

'No, that's what I told him.'

'Wh—what you told him . . .?'

'Oh yes. That was the only reason he agreed to do the painting.'

'You mean he actually had the nerve to think that I—— The nerve of the man!'

'Not really. He's rather handsome, fascinating actually, women are always making fools of themselves over him. He just wanted to be sure you weren't in that category.'

'Well, I'm not,' Sophie said angrily, puting the denims

and sun-top back on over her briefs and bra in a gesture of defiance. Luke Vittorio could make what he wanted of her clothing.

'Oh, I assured him of that.' Rosemary went to the door. 'But please behave yourself this afternoon. Luke is a—a friend of mine.'

Sophie hadn't missed the slight hesitation before the word 'friend'. 'I'll be very polite to your—friend,' she retorted.

Her stepmother gave a sweet smile. 'I was going to come with you, at Luke's request, but I would find it boring watching him working all afternoon.'

'I see.' Sophie looked at her wrist-watch. 'I'd better be leaving. I wouldn't want to be late.'

'No, Luke dislikes unpunctuality.'

Damn Luke and what he liked or disliked! Sophie was tempted to tell the taxi-driver to take a detour so that she was deliberately late, but the desire passed as she thought of arriving at Luke Vittorio's apartment only to be refused admission owing to her lateness.

She was obviously expected; her name acted like magic as the lift was called for her. She had the feeling that she would have been politely but firmly ejected if her name hadn't been on the commissionaire's list. Still, it was only natural that someone of Luke Vittorio's fame would want to protect his privacy.

The lift zoomed up to the top floor with startling rapidity, much more quickly than Sophie would have wished for. She wasn't looking forward to this, she wasn't looking forward to it at all.

She stepped straight from the lift into a luxurious reception room, although she didn't linger to take in the complete luxury of the deep-pile carpets and leather furniture. She could hear the soft strains of music and as her host hadn't put in an appearance yet it seemed logical to conclude that he was where the music was.

It wasn't very polite of him not to greet her, but then she had never encouraged politeness from him. She let herself into the room adjoining this one, registering that it was just as well furnished and was probably his main sitting-room. Several doors led off this room, although there was nothing to tell her which room the music was coming from. She felt slightly ridiculous, but there seemed only one way to detect which room had the movement in, and that was by listening at the doors. She didn't want to just open the doors, he could be doing anything.

'Are you listening for woodworm?' drawled that husky accented voice from behind her as she leant on a door. 'If so I think I should tell you that this apartment does not have it.'

Sophie spun round guiltily, feeling like an eavesdropper caught in the act. Her eyes widened as she took in his appearance, the snug-fitting black trousers and the hastily pulled on loose-fitting white silk shirt. His dark hair had a damp look to it and the shirt was completely open at the front, giving the impression that he had just showered and had been in the process of dressing.

Sophie found the shirt fascinating, never having actually seen anyone wearing one like it before. It didn't appear to have any buttons, merely wrapped over but still revealing a great deal of bare chest, to be tucked into the narrow waistband of his trousers. The sleeves were long and full, caught at the wrists by a single pearl button, and the whole effect should have been feminine, but on this man it just seemed to emphasise his maleness.

'Well?' He tucked in the remainder of his shirt.

Sophie realised she must look foolish, gaping at him like this, but he was devastatingly handsome, so handsome he unnerved her completely. 'I—er—I didn't know which room you would be in,' she explained lamely.

He nodded, turning back into the room he had just left. 'So you decided to listen at keyholes.'

'I did no such thing!' She walked into the room too, backing out as she realised it was his bedroom. 'Well . . . not the way you put it!'

He shrugged, switching off the radio before brushing his dark hair. 'Then what would you call it?'

'I—— You weren't in the other room to meet me,' she said angrily. 'How was I supposed to know what to do?'

'You could have waited until I came through.'

'I could have done, but I had no way of knowing if you knew of my arrival.'

Luke came into the sitting-room, closing the bedroom door behind him. 'I was taking a shower when Sam called up, hence my undress just now.'

'Well, I wasn't to know that,' Sophie told him tartly, still very much aware of how attractive he looked in that strange-looking shirt. 'Anyway, where are your servants, they could have let me in.'

'I do not have any.'

'You—— You mean we're here alone?'

His dark eyes gleamed with mocking humour. 'Does that bother you?'

Of course it bothered her! 'I—well, I just didn't expect it,' she pushed back her long straight blonde hair selfconsciously. 'I assumed you would at least have a cook and someone to clean for you.'

'I am perfectly capable of doing my own cooking when necessary, and I have a woman come in three times a week to clean for me. I sometimes keep strange hours, and I do not like being answerable to anyone for my actions.'

'I suppose it could be rather restricting.'

His eyes narrowed. 'I did not mean it was restricting, I

meant it is more convenient to me not to have to inform people of my arrivals and departures. I travel a great deal.'

'So I've noticed.'

'Then you can see my point of view.'

'Oh, I see it, I just find it unusual. You don't appear to me to be the type of man who would enjoy catering for yourself.'

'I will not ask what type of man you think me to be,' he said dryly. 'You have made your opinion of me perfectly clear. Would you like to come into the studio now?' he invited.

Sophie followed him into a room that couldn't be mistaken for anything other than what it was. Canvases stood about the room, landscapes, portraits, others just bare but waiting for the master touch. Sophie found it all fascinating, the smell of the paint, the much simpler furnishing in here—only scatter rugs, a sofa and one armchair, the easel with a prepared canvas and the table next to it with paints and brushes on its surface. Huge windows dominated the two outside walls, the room was full of light, as she presumed it needed to be.

'Would you like to lie on the sofa?' Luke was already intent on arranging things on the table top.

Sophie spluttered with laughter. 'You surely aren't going to have me in the typical reclining position?'

'I am not going to *have* you in any position,' he said abruptly. 'Now, if you will please get on the sofa.'

She did so, her face fiery red. She sat upright, her body rigid. 'I didn't mean—— I wasn't implying that——'

'I know you were not,' he came over to her. 'But at least I have momentarily stopped your glib answers.' He put a hand on her shoulder. 'Could you try to relax? I am not about to leap on you simply because we are alone. Lie back, tuck your legs up beneath you. That is better.' He moved back to the easel.

She had done as he said like an automaton, his hands seeming to burn her where he touched. He was right, she had run out of glib answers, but mainly because his closeness, the fresh cleanness of him, his tangy aftershave all contrived to make her tongue-tied.

'Could you lean a little to the right, Sophie?' He was considering her with completely clinical eyes. 'That's better. Your face to the right also.'

For the next ten minutes he changed her position numerous times, finally settling for her gazing out of the window slightly to the right of him, one leg bent up beneath her, the other stretched the length of the sofa.

'Do you think it will take long?' She held her head stiffly to the right as he had told her, already feeling the muscles beginning to tense at the back of her neck.

Luke shrugged. 'That will depend on how co-operative you are. You are much too tense already.'

Her violet eyes flashed. 'I can't help that, this isn't a very comfortable position.'

'It is not meant to be, no one said you would be comfortable.' He drew strong outlines on the canvas with charcoal. 'Just relax, forget you are posing. Talk if it helps, it will not trouble me.'

'And what would I talk about?' Sophie wished she could look at him instead of just being able to see his slight movements to the left of her vision.

'Anything or nothing, I do not mind.'

She was sure he didn't, his concentration fully on the canvas in front of him. 'Do you see my stepmother often?' She wanted to shake him out of his complacency.

His concentration didn't falter. 'Occasionally.'

'How often is occasionally?' she probed. 'Once a week, twice a week, more?'

'I do not keep a record.'

'She wanted to come here today, didn't she?'

'Did she?'

'You know she did. You asked her to come,' she accused, her mouth set stubbornly.

'Did I?'

She turned her head. 'You know you did!'

Luke sighed impatiently. 'Will you please sit still. How do you expect me to be able to work if you do nothing but move about?'

Sophie regained the pose with ill-humour. 'You're just avoiding answering the question.'

He moved with angry movements. 'I am not!' He wrenched her chin round, his eyes blazing into hers. 'You are not here to ask questions but to pose while I paint. I see your mother perhaps twice a week. Does that answer you?'

'I suppose so,' she muttered, her jaw clamped between his long fingers. 'Would you let go of me, you're hurting.'

His teeth flashed whitely with devilish humour. 'Do not worry, I will not paint in the bruises.'

'I haven't noticed you've done much of anything so far,' she snapped.

'That is because you do not look as you should. There is something missing, something about you . . . Ah, I know what it is.'

'You—you do?' She tried to look away from the expression in his eyes, but he held her immovable.

'Mm,' he knelt on the sofa beside her. 'The passion is missing from your eyes.'

'The—the passion?' she gulped.

'The passion we spoke of at our last meeting,' he murmured softly, druggingly. 'Are you deliberately holding that back from me?'

'Don't be ridiculous! I don't know what you're talking about.' She struggled against him.

'But you do.' His hand left her chin to encircle her

throat, his thumb gently caressing her skin. 'Your eyes are almost purple at this moment,' he said huskily.

Sophie gulped again, more than a little frightened by the feelings he was arousing within her, feelings she didn't think she should be feeling.

'Yes, purple,' he continued throatily. 'Why is that?'

'I——' she cleared her throat, 'I don't know.'

'I do.' He bent his dark head to claim her lips.

He took his time, savouring each movement of their lips, his tongue moving caressingly along the edge of her bottom lip. Sophie sank back against the cushions, taking Luke with her. He felt weightless above her, those long tapered hands running slowly over the contours of her body, their kiss lengthening and deepening.

Sophie's body felt on fire, straining against him as passion mounted, her arms about his neck as she held him to her. She had never been kissed so intimately before, never felt the hard contours of a man's body so close to her own, his arousal as evident as her own.

His face buried in her throat she gasped for breath. 'Why are my eyes purple, Luke? Why?'

'Because of that passion I keep talking about.'

'No,' she shook her head dazedly. 'No!'

'Oh yes, Sophie,' he raised his head to look at her. 'You should not be ashamed of such feelings, but rather rejoice that you are able to feel this way; many women are not so lucky.'

'And you would know, wouldn't you?' she accused, sanity returning.

A coldness entered his eyes and he began to move away. 'Yes, I would know.'

Sophie sat up, straightening her hair with shaking fingers. 'I'm sorry, I shouldn't have said that.'

'You should if you believe it to be true.' He moved back to stand in front of the easel, tucking the loose shirt back into his trousers, the gesture reminding Sophie of how she had touched and caressed his bare chest only seconds earlier. 'We will continue,' he said curtly.

'We will continue . . .?'

'Yes.' He picked up the charcoal. 'You have exactly the right expression on your face now. You will see it is true what I said, coolness outside belied by the passion hidden in your eyes.'

Sophie was very pale. 'You—you did that on purpose! You kissed me to—to get an effect for your painting!' Her voice had risen shrilly.

His expression was enigmatic. 'Why else?'

'Why else indeed?' she echoed angrily, standing up. 'And do you kiss all the women you paint?'

'Some of them, if the situation merits it.'

She walked angrily to the door. 'I don't think this situation merited it, Mr Vittorio. In fact, I think you're very much mistaken about me. I don't enjoy being kissed for an experiment.' Especially as she had responded!

'Come now,' he taunted softly. 'You enjoyed it as much as I did. There is nothing wrong in enjoying the pleasure our own bodies can give us. Admit you enjoyed it.'

'I admit nothing!' She swung open the door.

'Where do you think you are going?'

'Back to my stepmother's apartment. You haven't forgotten my stepmother?' she scorned.

'No,' he replied calmly, 'I have not forgotten her. What does she have to do with my kissing you?'

'What does she——! You're disgusting!' she cried. 'How you can stand there and ask me such a question is beyond me!'

He walked towards her with long furious strides, wrenching the door out of her hands to slam it shut. 'A lot of things are beyond you at this time! But then you have a lot against you—your youth, your impetuosity, this habit you have of jumping to conclusions,' there could be no doubt he was very angry. 'Go back to the sofa, Sophie, and resume your pose. I have not finished for today yet.'

'I——'

'Do it, Sophie,' he ordered grimly. 'Before I resume making love to you. At the moment I could do one of three things—make love to you, beat you, or simply continue with the portrait. I would prefer to do the latter. You have your choice.'

Sophie went jerkily back to the sofa and resumed her pose, more out of cowardice than anything else. She had no doubt he would carry out his threat, and she didn't particularly want either of the former to happen.

Luke took up his position behind the canvas, working with a speed and concentration she felt glad of. Nothing had prepared her for that kiss, not his blatant masculinity or the magnetism of his eyes. She had simply melted under his expert seduction, offering no resistance to his more intimate caresses of her body.

'Do not frown,' he said curtly.

'I wasn't aware that I was,' she flushed.

'That is why I told you.'

'Couldn't we stop now?' She flexed her aching muscles. 'We've been here for hours now.'

'Two, to be precise,' he mocked. 'Just a few minutes more and we will stop.'

Sophie sighed. 'All right.'

'Tell me, why do you bother to wear a bra?'

She gave him a sharp look, instantly wanting to cover her breasts from his eagle eye. 'What sort of question is that to ask someone?' she snapped to cover her embarrassment.

He shrugged, wiping his hands on a cloth beside him before standing back to look at his work. 'It is a relevant one.'

'But very personal.'

'You consider it too personal?'

She swallowed hard. 'That depends, on your reason for asking it.'

'Curiosity, nothing more.'

'Why do most women wear one?' she dismissed.

'Because they are ashamed of their body. You have nothing to be ashamed of.'

She couldn't meet his eyes. 'How do you know that?'

'Your muscle tone, the natural shape of you. I would prefer that you do not wear one the next time you sit for me.'

'Couldn't you just imagine it? I've always——' she broke off as he began to laugh. 'What do you find so funny?'

'You,' he chuckled softly. 'You have asked me to imagine you without your bra, when I have been doing nothing else all afternoon.'

'You . . .' she gulped.

Luke nodded. 'That sun-top is very provocative.'

'Yes, but you—well, you shouldn't be——'

'I should not be looking at you as a man but as a painter,' he finished wryly. 'I find it impossible to separate the two where you are concerned.'

'Oh!'

'You are surprised. Come, I will make us some coffee and stop embarrassing you.' He held the door open for her.

'Can't I see what you've done so far?' she asked.

'No. Come.'

She followed him with ill-humour. 'Aren't you going to let me see it at all?'

'No.'

Sophie watched him move about the kitchen making the coffee. 'Not at all?'

'No,' he repeated.

She sighed. 'Do you always work this way?'

'No,' he said again, handing her a mug of steaming

coffee. 'I have a feeling that your portrait is going to be the best thing I have ever done.'

'Really?' They were seated in the lounge, Sophie in an armchair and Luke sprawled on the sofa, his long legs stretched out in front of him, the silk shirt open even further in his relaxed state to reveal more of his strong muscular chest.

'I hope so,' he said.

'Why do you think that?'

'For the reason I have already stated, your coolness and fire will come alive, I hope, under my brush.'

She shook her head. 'I'm sure no one else sees me as you do.'

His gaze ran lingeringly over her body. 'Perhaps not. You show me a side of your nature I would wish no one else to see.'

Sophie shifted uncomfortably. 'You bring out the worst in me.'

'That was not the side I meant,' he drawled throatily.

She got up jerkily. 'I think I'd better leave now.'

Luke stood up too, moving with all the languid grace of which he was capable. 'You will not stay to dinner?'

Sophie looked down at her denims and sun-top. 'Not dressed like this.'

'There is no one to see you here but me.'

That was what she was afraid of. 'I'm sure you must have another appointment, especially as it's a Saturday night.'

He came towards her. 'It is something I can put off.'

She gave a shaky laugh. 'Not for me, please.'

Luke stood directly in front of her now, holding her close to him simply by the look in his eyes. 'There is much I would do for you if you would let me.'

'Oh,' she blinked rapidly in an effort to break from his spell. 'I—er—I really think I should leave.'

'If that is your wish,' he nodded haughtily, moving away. 'You will be here the same time next Saturday.'

'Is that an order or a request?' she bridled.

He raised dark eyebrows. 'What do you think?'

'The former.'

'The same time next week,' he didn't dispute her answer. 'And I will endeavour to be dressed. But remember, no bra.'

She blushed. 'I most certainly——'

'No bra, Sophie,' he ordered. 'You do not need it.'

'Is there anything else about me you aren't satisfied with?' she asked tartly.

'Do not tempt me,' he taunted.

'*That* I have no intention of doing. Goodbye, Mr Vittorio.'

He watched her go with mocking eyes, a tall lithe man who could wind any woman round his little finger with his Latin charm, including herself. She couldn't believe she had actually let him kiss her, had *enjoyed* it. It was simply the natural reaction to the advances of a seductive charm, she told herself, nothing more.

She took her time going back to her stepmother's apartment, deciding to walk instead of getting a taxi. When she finally arrived it was well after seven, and her stepmother was obviously ready to go out to dinner.

'Going anywhere nice?' Sophie hadn't expected Rosemary to be going out this evening too, although she supposed it was too much to ask to expect her stepmother to change her routine because of her.

'Dinner and a show,' Rosemary said smugly. 'The play is sure to be good, Luke has excellent taste.'

Sophie paled. 'You're going with Luke Vittorio?'

Her mother patted her hair into place, blotting her scarlet lipstick.

'That's right.' she kissed Sophie on the cheek. 'Don't wait up for me, I'll probably be very late.'

'Have a nice time,' Sophie said dully.

It wasn't the fact that her stepmother was going out with Luke Vittorio that dazed her, it was the fact that he had been willing to cancel it in order to have dinner with *her*. She wondered what game he was playing with them.

CHAPTER FOUR

SHE wondered the same thing the next time she saw him. He was once again mildly flirtatious, and she knew he had noted her lack of a bra at the first glance. She felt very selfconscious about it, but he appeared to have no such inhibitions, his eyes deepening appreciatively as they ran over her.

He was dressed exactly the same, the fitted black trousers and the flamboyant white shirt, and he had kept his word and been dressed when Sophie arrived.

He was studying her now, his look critical. 'You look tired today,' he said abruptly.

Sophie instantly felt the colour enter her cheeks. 'Thank you!' she snapped. She knew very well what she looked like. She had been to a dinner-dance with Nicholas the previous evening and hadn't got to bed until after three o'clock this morning, and the train journey up here had seemed extra long today too, probably because she was already so tired.

'Why do you look tired?'

In the same pose of last week she couldn't look at him,

feeling at a disadvantage. 'I do have a social life, you know.'

'You were out last night. With Nicholas, I suppose?'

'Yes.' Her lips clamped together.

'You intend marrying him?'

This time she did look at him. 'What does that have to do with you?'

Luke shrugged. 'Nothing, of course. Your stepmother merely mentioned——'

'Let's leave my stepmother out of this!'

'If you wish,' he nodded. '*Are* you going to marry him?'

'I——'

'He would not be right for you.' He put down his brush and came over to stand in front of her, his muscular thighs on a level with her eyes. 'You need someone much stronger, so that the man would dominate, not you.'

'I don't dominate,' she denied huskily, wrenching her gaze away from his body and up to his face, wishing she hadn't when she saw the intimacy in his eyes.

He gave a slow smile and sat down beside her on the sofa. 'Not me perhaps, but you dominate that poor boy.'

'He isn't a boy!' she flashed.

One long slender hand moved to caress her golden hair. 'Is he not?' he said thoughtfully. 'He is your lover, perhaps?'

'Certainly not!' she cried indignantly, cursing the way her heart leapt at his touch.

'He is not?'

'No!'

'Why so vehement?' His thumb ran caressingly over her parted lips. 'You are nineteen, you mix with people constantly involved in one affair or another, so it is natural to assume you are the same. Also, your body enjoys being touched.'

Sophie could have told him that no other man touched

her the way he did, but at the moment something else he had said seemed more important to her. This man was having an affair with her stepmother, made no secret of the fact, and yet he wasn't averse to flirting with her too. He was despicable!

She jerked away from his caressing hand. 'You think I'm promiscuous?'

'Not promiscuous, merely aware of physical pleasure.'

'Doesn't that amount to the same thing?' she asked tartly.

'Not at all. I find you—intriguing, Sophie,' he told her slowly, his hands on her forearms now.

'Please, not again!' She squirmed under his touch.

Luke frowned. 'Not again—what?'

'Please, don't kiss me again to get the effect for your painting. I—I don't want you to kiss me,' she lied.

'But it would not be for the portrait,' he told her softly.

Sophie raised startled eyes. 'It—it wouldn't?'

'No,' he groaned, bending his head to caress her throat with firm lips. 'This time it would be for myself alone.'

'You——'

'Do not talk, Sophie,' he ordered abruptly. 'Not if you are going to object. I want you, desire you, and I believe you want me too.'

His mouth on her throat was doing strange things to her resistance. Who was she kidding? she didn't have any resistance to this man. 'I——' her voice came out in a squeak. 'That isn't true,' she said firmly.

His fingers pressed gently on her lips. 'I asked you not to speak if you were going to object,' he reminded her throatily.

'But I——'

'Not now, Sophie,' he said with a groan. 'Kiss me.'

'No!'

'Kiss me!'

She couldn't do anything other than obey the command in his dark brooding eyes, and lifted her mouth for his kiss. But he had no intention of being the one to do the kissing; he left the initiative up to her.

After the first tentative touch she had no hesitation in doing so, her lips being the ones to part and deepen the kiss, her hands on his bare chest beneath his shirt. Luke gave a low growl of triumph before lowering her back against the cushions, the master now.

Each kiss was more drugging than the last, each touch more intimate. Luke's hands were beneath the thin material of her cotton blouse, dangerously close to her breasts and yet not quite touching them as they strained against the confining material.

She slipped the shirt from his shoulders, watching the ripple of muscle as he discarded it altogether, his chest and arms deeply brown and covered with a fine mat of hair that she felt sure went way past his navel.

Luke's fingers moved with experience as he quickly dispatched with the tiny mother-of-pearl buttons on the front of her blouse, bending his dark head to caress her aroused nipples with sensuous lips, his tongue hardening them to full pulsating peaks.

Suddenly he stood up to scoop her up into his arms, his mouth taking control of hers as he strode through the apartment. Sophie felt herself lowered gently on to the bed before he joined her, his aroused body half lying over her, more seductive than any words. He slipped the blouse from her heated body, feasting his eyes on her bare breasts.

His hand moved to cup and caress one creamy breast, his fingertips evoking such pleasure that she gasped. 'I knew you would look like this,' he moaned, touching her nipple. 'Made for love,' he smoothed the skin. 'A body made for love.'

Sophie was lost, lost in the intimacy of the situation, in

the sensuousness that was Luke, knowing there could be only one end to this. And she wanted it to happen, wanted it desperately. 'Luke——'

'Quiet!' he ordered, turning towards the open doorway. 'There is someone in the apartment.' He stood up in one fluid movement.

Her eyes were dazed. 'Someone . . .'

'Yes!' he snapped, pulling on a bathrobe over his naked chest, his shirt still in the studio. 'Stay here. I will not be long.'

Once he had gone Sophie scrambled to her feet, the mood broken. Who on earth would dare to just walk into his home in this way? Her stepmother would!

She softly eased the door open and was just in time to see her stepmother walk into the lounge, Luke's composure perfect as he greeted her. There didn't seem to be anything very intimate about their greeting, although that was probably due to the fact that Luke was conscious of her presence in his bedroom.

'I came to collect Sophie,' Rosemary smiled.

'Sophie?' Luke echoed sharply, obviously not as controlled as he looked. 'She is not here.'

'Not here? But—well, it's early yet. I thought——'.

'She said she had some shopping to do,' he cut in grimly.

'The naughty child!' her stepmother chided with a smile. 'I hope she isn't being tiresome, she can be so obstinate at times.'

'Sophie's behaviour has been perfectly—satisfactory.'

Rosemary gave him a sharp look. 'Are you all right, Luke? You look a little pale.'

'I am fine,' he ran a hand through his thick dark hair. 'I was just going to take a shower when you arrived.'

'Really?' her stepmother said throatily.

'Yes,' he said sharply. 'I—er—I hope you do not mind, Rosemary, but I am feeling a little tired.'

'You work too hard,' she scolded gently. 'Why don't you come down to the house next weekend? You could work down there and it would give you a rest. I'm sure we could convert one of the rooms for you to use.'

'Perhaps,' he nodded.

'Oh, do come,' she encouraged. 'I'm sure Simon would love to see you again.'

'It is only two weeks since we last met,' he reminded her dryly.

'Yes, but we had a houseful of people then. Come alone this time and we'll have just family.'

'I am hardly a member of your family, Rosemary.'

She gave a husky laugh. 'No, that's true.'

'My shower, Rosemary,' he reminded her curtly.

'Oh yes.' She moved to the door. 'But you will think about next weekend? Let me know tonight, hmm?'

He nodded. 'Very well.'

Sophie softly closed the door and leaned back against it, her breathing ragged. So Luke was seeing her stepmother again this evening. How could he make love to her this afternoon and then go to Rosemary tonight! She didn't doubt for one moment that they would be together in this bedroom now if it weren't for her own presence here.

She was buttoning her blouse with shaking fingers when Luke came back into the bedroom. 'What are you doing?' he asked throatily, his dark eyes intent on her.

She didn't bother to look at him. 'Leaving,' she mumbled.

'There is no need, we are alone again.'

'There's no need——!' She glared at him. 'There's every need! That was my stepmother out there.'

'I do not see——'

'And she walked in here as if she was used to doing so. And we both know why, don't we?' she accused shrilly.

His eyes narrowed. 'Do we?'

'Oh yes,' she scorned, brushing past him. 'Excuse me, I'm leaving now.'

'We have done nothing to the portrait today.'

'Is that my fault?' she demanded. 'It will have to wait, I'm certainly not in the mood for that now.'

'Neither am I,' he said meaningly. 'Next weekend I will——'

'You'll be joining us in the country,' she finished for him. 'I know.'

'Listening at doors again?' he taunted.

'I do not listen at doors! Well . . . only this once,' she conceded. 'I just hope you remember what I told you about my father. I won't have him hurt.' She collected her handbag from the studio, Luke's silk shirt lying on the floor reminding her of the intimacies she had just shared with this man.

He was standing in the lounge when she turned to leave and her cheeks coloured anew. His mouth turned back with taunting humour as if he were perfectly well aware of the thoughts going through her mind. Sophie gave him one last furious glare before slamming out of the apartment.

This couldn't go on, this being made love to by a man she despised. She had heard of the power of physical attraction, but never thought she would become its victim. But she was definitely in Luke Vittorio's clutches, a mere puppet while he pulled the strings. And he knew it, he knew that physically he was capable of brushing aside any objections she might make. Her own acceptance of it left her feeling vunerable, very vulnerable.

Her stepmother was in the lounge taking tea when she arrived back at the apartment, and she poured out a cup wordlessly for Sophie. 'You don't appear to have bought anything,' she remarked slowly, her blue eyes narrowed.

Sophie frowned. 'Sorry?'

'Luke said you'd gone shopping. You don't seem to have bought anything.'

'Oh—oh, no,' her face was scarlet. She wondered what her stepmother would say if she told her that far from being shopping, only seconds before her own unannounced appearance in the apartment she had been in Luke's bedroom being thoroughly kissed. She sipped her tea hurriedly, burning her mouth in the process. 'I—I didn't see anything I liked.'

'You don't like Luke either, do you?'

Sophie hesitated. She didn't like him, but could she honestly say she *dis*liked someone who could affect her so much physically? 'He's too forceful,' she said finally.

Rosemary smiled to herself. 'Yes, he is, isn't he? I do like a man to be strong.'

'Daddy's strong,' Sophie said resentfully.

'I know that,' her stepmother snapped. 'But Luke is— well, he's different.'

'He's a flirt and a womaniser!'

'They are one and the same thing,' Rosemary laughed huskily. 'And of course he is, but it doesn't mean anything. I wouldn't be surprised if he's even flirted with you.'

Sophie clamped her lips together. She wouldn't call the intimacies she had shared with Luke Vittorio 'flirtation'. He had been intent on making love to her, and fool that she was, she had been letting him.

'Has he?' Rosemary probed.

'Has he what?' she mumbled into her tea-cup.

Again she gave that husky laugh. 'Flirted with you.'

Sophie flung her head back defiantly. 'And if he has?' she challenged. 'Would you be jealous?'

Her stepmother's blue eyes narrowed. 'What sort of question is that to ask me?'

'A very pertinent one, I would have thought. *Would* you be jealous?'

'As far as Luke is concerned I have nothing to feel jealous about. Every woman is a challenge to him, once he's conquered them he's no longer interested. For example, Eve Jeffers is a thing of the past.'

'So you don't consider any woman a threat?'

Rosemary smiled coyly. 'A threat to what, Sophie?'

'To the affair you're having with the man!' she said disgustedly.

Her stepmother patted the perfection of her hair. 'And who says I'm having an affair with him?'

'It's obvious.'

'Is it? I wasn't aware of it.'

'You don't exactly try to hide it,' Sophie said bitterly. 'How would you like it if Daddy behaved in the same way?'

Rosemary smiled. 'Your father would never do such a thing.'

'No, he wouldn't,' Sophie agreed dully. Her father would do anything for a quiet life, an affair would be a complication he didn't need. And her stepmother knew it, knew just how to manage and manipulate him. As she and Joycy had surmised at the last big display of tears two weeks ago, Rosemary had wheedled a magnificent pair of drop-diamond ear-rings out of him.

'You still haven't answered my original question,' her stepmother prompted.

'I've forgotten what it was,' Sophie evaded, forgetting nothing at all.

Her stepmother smiled as if she knew very well she hadn't. 'Has Luke been flirting with you?'

'He may have been. But I can't stand him,' she added hurriedly. 'And I don't know how you can like him when he can behave like that with your own stepdaughter.'

'Are *you* jealous, Sophie?'

'Certainly not! I think the whole thing is disgusting.'

'But you aren't trying too hard to resist him,' Rosemary said with a laugh.

'I——'

'Admit it, Sophie, he's irresistible. At least, I've always found him so.'

'Don't you feel in the least guilty about cheating on Daddy?'

Rosemary stood up. 'Don't try to interfere in things you can't possibly understand. And don't read too much into Luke's advances to you, they don't mean a thing.'

Her stepmother sounded very sure about that, and yet they hadn't merely been advances. She might even still be with him now if it hadn't been for Rosemary's interruption.

'Do sit down, Sophie,' Rosemary snapped. 'You've been jumping in and out of that chair for the last hour.'

Sophie was well aware of that. All morning the staff had been clearing the room next to Luke's bedroom for his use as a studio, and now they were just waiting for him to arrive.

She hadn't been at all surprised when Rosemary had arrived the previous evening and informed her father that Luke would be coming down for the weekend; she had expected him to take advantage of the invitation.

She sprang up out of the chair again. 'I think I'll go and see Helen.'

'You most certainly will not,' her stepmother said sharply. 'Luke's coming here to paint you.'

'Yes, but—well, he isn't my guest.'

'Simon,' Rosemary snapped, 'talk some sense into this girl!'

He sighed. 'It would look a bit strange if you were out, poppet. You are his reason for being here.'

Oh no, she wasn't! She glared her resentment at her stepmother. 'But he can't possibly want to start work as soon as he arrives. I'll only be gone an hour or so.'

'She's right, you know, Rosemary. He may not want to start until tomorrow.'

'Oh, very well,' Rosemary gave in with ill-grace. 'But make sure it is only an hour.'

Sophie ran up to her room to change before any more objections could be forthcoming. She felt more comfortable in her denims and tee-shirt, whistling happily to herself as she went out through the kitchen.

Joycy turned from her baking. 'Well, you sound happier than you did this morning.'

Sophie grinned. 'I'm being allowed out.'

Joycy laughed. 'You make this sound like a prison!'

'It's seemed like it today. See you later,' she called gaily.

Her bicycle had been mended by Martin, with much muttering from him that it was ready for the scrapheap. She swerved at the end of the driveway as a sleek car turned in. Oh no, not again!

Luke pressed the button to wind down the window. 'Good afternoon,' he greeted huskily, his dark gaze roaming over her appraisingly.

Sophie couldn't meet that look in his eyes. 'Hello.'

'Do you always ride about the countryside on a bicycle?' She shrugged. 'Why not?'

He smiled, a mocking smile. 'I would have thought that as the only daughter of a rich man you would have been speeding about these narrow roads in a sports car.'

She bristled angrily at his mockery. 'Oh, I have a sports car, it's in the garage. There's only one thing wrong with that—I can't drive.'

'You cannot drive?'

She laughed at his surprise. 'Just one of the things I dislike.'

'And I am another,' he taunted. 'Your mother and father are at home?'

'Oh yes, awaiting the arrival of their celebrated guest.'

'You did not feel the same necessity?'

Sophie shook her head. 'As I told them, you aren't my guest.'

Her rudeness seemed to pass unnoticed. 'Nevertheless,' he said softly, 'I am here to see you.'

'Are you?' she challenged.

'But of course.'

'I don't see any of course about it,' Sophie snapped. 'But don't worry, I'll make sure I'm available when you want to paint me. I just want to get it over with.' Her sitting for this portrait hadn't stopped Rosemary and this man meeting as she had hoped it would, in fact it had just made things worse; he seemed to think it gave him the right to make love to her too.

Luke gave a slow smile. 'It is nowhere near being completed. If you remember, last weekend we did nothing at all to it.'

Her face blushed scarlet. 'Oh yes,' she taunted, 'I'd forgotten you were trying to show me what a great lover you are. That's probably because it didn't work. You're accomplished, I'll give you that, but I think natural feeling is more important than experience.'

Luke laughed, her jibes obviously not affecting him. 'Does Nicholas give you this natural feeling?'

'Nicholas?' she looked startled. 'I haven't——'

'No, you have not,' he agreed. 'And I agree with you about feelings being more important than experience, but only because it is blatantly obvious to me that you do not have any of the latter. You pretend a sophistication that evaporates every time I touch you.'

'You conceited pig!'

'It is not conceit, Sophie. You dislike me and yet you let

me make love to you——'

'That's because of *your* experience,' she interrupted.

'It is because of your own desire,' he corrected. 'Admit it, Sophie, on a physical level we communicate perfectly.'

She gasped at his words, hating it being said even though she knew it to be true. 'I'm not staying here to listen to any more of this! I have more important things to do,' she lied.

'You are going to see Nicholas?'

'And if I am?'

He shrugged. 'I was merely curious. But I would not advise you to encourage him as you have encouraged me, it would merely frighten him.'

'I didn't encourage you!'

'Do not fool yourself, Sophie. I am merely warning you that Nicholas would be shocked by such emotion and desire as you display. It appeals to my Latin temperament, but he is a staid Englishman. If you marry him he will expect only children from you, not passion. His wife would have to be coolly responsive, not a raging inferno of emotions as you are.'

'I'm not——'

'I have kept you long enough. I will see you later.' He wound up the window in conclusion of the conversation.

Sophie was shaking with feeling. A raging inferno of emotions—was she really? Only when that man touched her. And she wasn't going to let him touch her again.

She changed her mind about going to Helen's and went to Nicholas's farm instead. He was out in one of the sheds when she arrived, much to her relief. She didn't really want to see his mother, not when she was feeling so confused.

Nicholas looked up from forking the hay, a smile of welcome on his face. 'You should have told me you were coming over,' he ran a hand down his mud-stained corduroys. 'I could at least have made an effort to be clean when you got here.'

She shrugged. 'It doesn't matter. I—er—All this makes you feel very close to nature. The sweet smell of hay, the sunshine blazing through the open doorway.'

He put down the pitchfork. 'I suppose so,' he replied, uncertain of her mood.

Sophie watched him walk over to the door. 'Where are you going?' She deliberately adopted a provocative pose, her voice low and inviting. Nicholas frowned, a dark hue beginning to appear in his cheeks. 'Up to the house. You can have tea while I change.'

'There's no need to change.' She swayed over to him putting her arms up about his neck. 'Shut the door, Nicholas.'

He looked at her as if she had gone mad, trying to pull her hands away.

'What's the matter with you?' he asked heatedly. 'Why are you acting so strangely?'

She pouted up at him. 'It isn't strange to want to be kissed. Close the door, Nicholas, and kiss me.'

'Kiss you? But——' he looked horrified, 'not out here, Sophie.'

She took his hand and led him over to the newly laid pile of hay. 'Right here, Nicholas.' She pulled him down beside her.

He visibly gulped. 'You—I—Are you quite well, Sophie?'

'Don't you want to kiss me?'

'Well, of course I do, but I——'

'Then kiss me—kiss me,' she ordered.

His mouth touched hers tentatively, drawing back slightly as her lips opened to deepen the kiss. He was kissing her with restrained passion, his body held rigidly away from her.

Sophie moved her mouth on his with fierce desperation, wanting to incite his desire for her, to spark a little savagery within him, but most of all she wanted to prove Luke Vittorio wrong, wanted to be able to say that Nicholas aroused her as much as he did.

But he didn't, and worse than that, Nicholas was shocked by her behaviour, really shocked. And he made her feel dirty and degraded for trying to force him into some show of emotion.

She wrenched out of his arms, standing up to brush her clothes down, studiously avoiding looking at him. 'I—I'm sorry,' she muttered. 'I'd better go.'

Nicholas stood up too, very red-faced. 'I—Sophie, why did you——'

'Forget it,' she snapped. 'I made a mistake, that's all.'

He grabbed at her arm as she turned away. 'Don't go yet, Sophie. You—well, you took me by surprise.' He went to pull her back into his arms. 'It will be different this time.'

She evaded his mouth, struggling against him. 'No, Nicholas! I said I made a mistake. I—I thought you wanted me.'

Again the colour entered his boyish face. 'I do! I want to marry you, you know that.'

'No! I have to go,' she said more calmly. 'We—we have Mr Vittorio down this weekend.'

'Can I come and see you later?' he asked hopefully.

She couldn't look at him, she was so ashamed of what she had just tried to do. 'I don't think that's a good idea. And I'm sorry about just now, I don't know why I did it.' Liar! She had done it because of Luke Vittorio's taunts.

'Sophie, please——'

'No!' She ran to the door. 'Please forget what happened. I don't think we should meet again.'

'You can't mean that. You've done nothing wrong, you just got carried away for a few minutes. I understand——'

She gave a harsh laugh. 'You can't possibly understand.' He couldn't understand the anger and humiliation that had prompted her to come here, couldn't understand that it was because of Luke Vittorio that she had been eager to be in his arms. 'Let me go, Nicholas!'

His hand fell away. 'If that's what you want.'

'It is.' She ran from the building.

She must have been mad, letting Luke Vittorio get under her skin so much that she had gone to Nicholas and made such an awful fool of herself. But at least it had proved one thing beyond doubt, Nicholas *was* shocked by her display of passion.

Her parents and Luke Vittorio were all seated in the lounge when she arrived home, her stepmother's eyebrows rising at her appearance in the room.

'What on earth have you been doing, Sophie? You look——'

'She looks as if she has been in a haystack,' Luke finished mockingly.

'Sophie?' her stepmother queried sharply.

She ran her hands through her ruffled hair. 'I'm just a little untidy, that's all.'

Luke stood up, his hand moving to her hair. 'Here,' he held out a piece of straw to her.

Sophie snatched it out of his hand. 'Thank you!' she glared at him.

'Helen telephoned earlier,' her father informed her. 'I thought you were going over there.'

'I—er—I went to see Nicholas instead,' she admitted with a quick glance at their guest.

Luke pulled another piece of straw out of her hair. 'I hope you did not shock him too much,' he taunted softly.

'Shut up!' she muttered vehemently.

'Stop whispering, you two!' Rosemary tried to sound teasing, but her voice came out rather shrill. 'Come and have some tea, Luke.'

Sophie excused herself, wanting a bath before she got ready for dinner. She was very aware of Luke's mockery towards her during the meal, and stayed away from him as much as she could. He knew exactly what had happened to her that afternoon, knew it and found it very amusing.

She went to her room as soon as it was polite to do so after dinner, unable to bear Luke's silent mockery any longer. She had no doubt that he would extract full satisfaction out of the situation when she sat for him tomorrow.

She woke with a jerk, sure that she hadn't just woken at random. She had heard a definite noise outside her door. She looked at the clock: one o'clock. Who on earth could be walking about at this time of night?—*creeping* about would be a better description.

She sat up with a start. Surely Rosemary wouldn't . . . Not in her own house! Sophie padded quickly over to the door, opening it with shaking fingers. She was just in time to see her stepmother disappearing around the end of the corridor, going in the direction of the two rooms Luke had been given.

Sophie hurriedly closed the door again, her breathing rapid. What should she do? Rosemary and her father had separate bedrooms, but that didn't mean her stepmother's absence wouldn't be detected. How could Rosemary be so damned stupid, how could she!

Sophie pulled on her wrap as she left her room, determined to put an end to this affair once and for all. She could hear the murmur of voices as she neared Luke's room, her mother's slightly raised, Luke's quietly soothing.

She didn't bother to knock, entering the room to see Rosemary in a seductive black négligé and Luke clothed only in a navy blue towelling robe, his bare legs visible beneath its knee-length. His dark hair was tousled, his brown eyes sleepy.

Her stepmother turned angry eyes on her. 'What are you doing here?' she snapped. 'As if I need to ask,' she sneered.

'What am *I* doing here?' Sophie choked. 'I followed *you*,' she accused.

'You aren't fooling anyone, Sophie. I've seen it, you see,' Rosemary cried. 'I've seen it!'

Sophie frowned, looking at Luke as if for understanding. 'Seen what? What have you seen?'

Her stepmother pulled her roughly to the side of the bed, throwing the cover back from the canvas that stood on the easel there. 'That!'

Sophie gasped as she looked at the painting of herself, not the portrait to hang in the family gallery as they had all imagined it to be, but a painting of her reclining on the sofa completely nude to the waist, the velvet shawl draped over her hips the same colour as her eyes. And what made it all the worse was the fact that Luke had painted in the tiny strawberry-coloured birthmark that was exactly over her heart.

She looked at him with dazed eyes. 'Luke . . .'

'Yes—Luke!' Rosemary sneered. 'I had no idea what would happen when I suggested this painting. Luke should know better, and you, Sophie—I would have thought you had more sense than to give yourself to the first man to flatter you. And don't say you haven't, I've known you most of your life and I know about that birthmark.'

Sophie was pale with disbelief. 'I don't——'

'What the hell is going on here?' Her father stood in the open doorway.

'What are you doing in Luke's bedroom? Rosemary, Sophie?'

'I came in here and found——'

'Rosemary came in and found Sophie and myself in a rather compromising situation.' Luke spoke for the first time, moving forward to put his arm about Sophie's shoulders. 'I realise this is hardly the time or place, Simon, but I would like your permission to marry your daughter.'

CHAPTER FIVE

HER father paled. 'You can't mean it!'

'Of course he doesn't,' Rosemary said hysterically, her face flushed, her eyes fever-bright.

'But I do mean it,' Luke told them calmly, the only controlled person in the room.

The conversation was passing over Sophie's head, her gaze still fixed on the painting that stood in the corner of the room. It was a very damning painting, giving her the look of a woman who had just been made love to.

The curve of her body was provocative in itself, but she was reaching forward slightly, her breasts twin peaks of invitation, the nipples thrust forward in full arousal. The face was definitely her too, but her expression was one of such—such blatant provocation, the lips parted poutingly, her eyes half closed as if guarding a great secret, that anyone looking at it could only come to one conclusion— she was a woman satiated by love and lovemaking.

She looked at Luke dazedly, but he was still looking at her father. How had he painted her looking like this? More to the point, *why* had he painted her like this?

'My God!' her father gasped as he saw the painting for

the first time, then he walked over to it, a look of disbelief in his eyes. Sophie could see the pain in his face as he turned back to look at her. 'Sophie?' his voice came out in a choked whisper.

She swallowed hard. 'I——'

'Sophie is not to blame,' Luke spoke again. 'She did not know of the painting either.'

Her father's face was flushed with anger as he looked at the younger man. 'It isn't a question of whether or not she knew of it, I want to know whether she *sat* for it, whether you've actually seen my daughter—my daughter *naked* like this!'

'Whether I have or have not——'

'The birthmark, Simon,' her stepmother interrupted. 'It's exactly right.'

'My God!' her father groaned again, slumping down on the bed. 'I can't believe it,' he ran a tired hand over his eyes. 'I just can't believe it!'

Sophie shook off Luke's arm and ran to kneel at her father's feet, her eyes pleading. 'It wasn't like that, Daddy,' she clutched at his hand. 'I—Luke—We——' What could she say? It wasn't like it looked, but there was no denying that Luke had seen the birthmark over her heart, that he had perhaps seen some of the provocative invitation shown in the painting too.

'We may have been slightly impetuous,' Luke finished for her. 'But love has a way of making one do these things.' His shrug was pure Latin in origin.

'You're in love with Sophie?' her stepmother demanded.

Luke met the sneer in Rosemary's eyes with cool haughtiness. 'Have I not just said so?'

'No, you——'

'For goodness' sake, Rosemary,' her husband snapped. 'If Sophie has—if things have gone this far between them,' he waved a hand vaguely in the direction of the painting, 'then of course they must be in love. Sophie isn't promiscuous and never has been.' He stood up. 'I think tempers are a little frayed,' he said in a more controlled voice. 'This could be better discussed in the morning, when we're all a little less heated.'

'I think you are right,' Luke nodded agreement. 'This is not the way I would have wished you to know of my desire to marry your daughter.'

'No,' Simon gave a strained smile. 'It's been a shock, but I understand—at least, I think I do.'

'Well, I don't,' his wife said shrilly. 'That painting is absolutely disgusting!' Her nose wrinkled with distaste. 'I trust you weren't about to sell it to us, Luke.'

'Hardly,' he said mockingly. 'The family portrait is in the other room, this one was meant for me alone.'

'Then why bring it down here?' she demanded.

'I was hoping to complete it tomorrow.'

'But——'

'Leave it, Rosemary,' her husband ordered. 'Let's get to bed while there's still some night left. Be back in your room in five minutes, Sophie,' he added sternly. 'No matter what may have passed before, you are not staying in here with Luke.'

She kept her head bowed. 'No, Daddy.'

'You're surely not leaving them here alone, Simon?' her stepmother demanded stubbornly.

'Come along, Rosemary,' he steered her firmly out of the room. 'It's a little late in the day to be worrying about Sophie's reputation.'

'Really, Simon, we can't just——'

'Not now, Rosemary,' and he closed the door behind them.

Sophie could still hear her stepmother protesting, although their voices were becoming weaker as they went back to their own bedrooms. She looked up at Luke. 'Why did you do it?' she choked, her misery a tangible thing.

'I have already explained that the painting was not meant for any other eyes but my own.'

'I didn't necessarily mean the painting, I meant all of it. It's bad enough that *that* should exist,' she blushed as she once again looked at the likeness of herself, 'but that you should tell my father we want to get married . . .!'

'What else could I have told him? That your stepmother did not find us here together but that it was the other way round, his wife and myself?' His eyes were chillingly cruel. 'Which do you think would have hurt him more, his daughter in my bedroom or his wife?'

She swallowed hard, feeling sick. 'But marriage . . .!'

'A little drastic perhaps, but the only thing that would placate your father in such a situation. You are an only child, the apple of your father's eyes, so to speak, he would not be able to accept such evidence of our lovemaking without knowing it was to be legalised.'

'But we haven't——' she broke off, embarrassed.

'No,' he agreed mockingly. 'But the painting tells another story.'

Sophie forced herself to look at it, at this stripping of her very soul until she felt she held nothing back from him. 'How did you——' she took a deep breath. 'How do you——'

'How do I know you will look like this after lovemaking?' He shrugged. 'Imagination is a wonderful thing. And it is not all imagination,' he added throatily. 'As your stepmother was quick to notice, some of it is all too lifelike.'

Like the birthmark on her left breast! 'And what do we tell them in the morning? How do we explain——'

'Explain what?' he cut in harshly.

'That you don't want to marry me.'

'I am not averse to the idea.'

'Well, I am!' she said indignantly. 'You aren't my idea of a husband. You—you're totally immoral, have women by the dozen.'

'Hardly the dozen, Sophie,' he mocked. 'And what else do you suggest we do? The last time I was here you told me I was never to hurt your father, and I am endeavouring not to do so. I could have told him the truth, but I think by doing so I would have been ridiculing a man I respect and admire. He perhaps allows his wife too much freedom, but——'

'And that's another thing,' she said heatedly. 'My step-mother came to your room tonight, would I be expected to take second place to her if I were your—your wife?' The word seemed to stick in her throat.

'There would be no other women unless you forced me into their arms,' he answered her coldly.

'What do you mean?'

'If I am kept satisfied in my own bed I will not seek out the pleasure to be found in others,' he told her calmly. 'A man rarely strays if he is finding fulfilment with his own wife.'

Sophie gulped. 'You mean you would expect me—that we would——'

'We would share a bed as well as a home,' he taunted. 'I could not live in such close proximity with a woman and not want her, and although we are not in love we do desire each other.'

'And how long would I have to stay married to you?' She didn't attempt to deny the desire, she would only be fooling herself if she did. She certainly wouldn't fool Luke!

'My religion does not allow divorce.'

'You mean—you mean it would be for ever?'

His mouth turned back. 'We could perhaps lead seperate lives if our desire ever becomes satiated. Do you doubt that I want you?'

One glance at the painting was enough to show her he did, it had been painted through the eyes of a man aroused and wanting. It made her blush to think of him experiencing such desire on her account. 'No,' she finally said huskily.

'Tell me, how did your experiment with Nicholas go this afternoon?'

Her mouth tightened at his mockery. 'Exactly as you said it would,' she admitted crossly.

'Englishmen do not have enough fire for you, Sophie,' Luke said seriously. 'We Italians do not spend our lives wondering about the flame of desire, we clasp it with both hands, even if we get burnt occasionally.'

She didn't need to be told of his prowess as a lover, she already knew it. 'And what happens when the flame goes out?' she asked.

He raised dark eyebrows. 'I do not envisage that happening between us.'

'But if it does?' she persisted.

'Come here,' he ordered throatily, pulling her roughly against the hard contours of his body. He slowly bent his head to tease her lips apart with the sensuous tip of his tongue, the open warmth of his mouth engulfing her as he had engulfed her once before, making her feel as one with him already.

She was breathless when he at last released her, looking very much as she did in the painting, she felt sure, completely wanton, in fact. 'Luke . . . Luke?' she questioned huskily. 'Is that really your name?' It didn't sound very Italian to her.

He nibbled her earlobe, feeling the shiver of pleasure that ran through her body. 'Luciano,' he supplied, looking down at her with teasing eyes. 'You expected it to be Lucifer, perhaps?'

Sophie blushed. 'No, I——'

He gave a throaty laugh, putting her away from him and securing his robe more securely about his waist. 'I am well aware of your antagonism to me on anything but a physical level, but it does not bother me.'

'Meaning you only want my body,' she snapped, stung by his attitude.

'I do not need to marry you to get that.' His face was a shuttered mask. 'We are marrying because after tonight your father expects it. The fact that we are not averse to each other is——'

'A bonus,' she sneered.

'I was not about to say that,' his voice became more accented in his anger. 'Oh, go to bed, Sophie. We can talk in the morning when you are feeling more reasonable.'

'There doesn't seem to be a lot left to say.' All the fight had gone out of her. 'I can't hurt my father, and the truth would do that.'

'I am glad you can see that.'

'Oh, I can see it, but whatever there was between you and my stepmother stops right now,' she added fiercely.

'Whatever there was has already stopped,' he said haughtily.

'And that—that painting, I don't want to see it again.'

'I do not think you are in a position to make conditions,' Luke said coolly. 'Although if it pleases you I will humour you in this one thing. But do not issue orders to me again, Sophie. You will find I react better to—persuasion.'

'Are you threatening me? Please me or I tell your father the truth?'

He looked at her coldly. 'I have no doubts about your pleasing me, you cannot help yourself. I was merely pointing out that you are not doing me any favours by becoming my wife, rather it is the other way round.'

He had her beaten and she knew it. 'I'll try never to

forget it,' she said sarcastically before slamming out of the room.

This was disastrous. She had followed her stepmother in all innocence and now found herself in a position where she was having to marry a man she barely knew, a man with plenty of sexual magnetism but no heart.

She slept fitfully, waking early to dress and go for a walk to try and clear her head. She loved the countryside around here and would miss it all when she and Luke were married and living in London. She hunched over in her depression, resigned to her fate but not welcoming it.

Life with Luke wasn't going to be easy, especially as she was weak towards him physically, but she could see no other solution to their problem. If her father knew what had really happened last night he would be hurt beyond healing. This way he was still hurt, but it was a hurt he would get over in time. Besides, there was the damning evidence of that painting.

She looked up as a horse and rider galloped across the field towards her, the rider known to her. Nicholas! She didn't know how she was going to face him after the exhibition she had made of herself yesterday.

He seemed to feel no embarrassment, as he jumped down from the horse's back to walk beside her. 'You're about early,' he smiled.

'I couldn't sleep,' she mumbled, her hands in the wide pockets of her navy blue skirt, the light blue blouse she wore complementing it perfectly. 'And it's such a lovely morning.' She had noticed that much even in her despair.

'I was going to call you last night,' his voice lowered intimately, 'but then I thought it would be better to come and see you today. I—I let you down yesterday and I want to explain.'

'Don't let's talk about it,' she interrupted hurriedly. 'I

don't know why I acted like that with you.'

'But we have to talk about it. I want to marry you, Sophie.'

'No!' she denied sharply.

He didn't seem to notice her shudder as he put his arm about her shoulders. 'But I do. I've always wanted to marry you, you know that.'

'You don't understand, Nicholas. I——'

'What Sophie is trying to say,' cut in a coldly angry voice, 'and not doing a very good job of it, I might add, is that she could not even contemplate marrying you when she has already consented to be *my* wife.'

Sophie looked at Luke with resignation. It was almost as if she had known he would interrupt them at this time, almost as if he had already taken over her life.

Nicholas looked astounded, his arm dropping away from her shoulders. 'You have to be kidding,' he said uncertainly.

Luke came to stand beside Sophie. 'Marriage is not something I would joke about. It is not a subject I find remotely amusing.'

Especially as the situation had been forced on them both. Sophie could understand Luke's anger.

Nicholas looked bewildered. 'But the two of you can't be getting married! Why, only yesterday——'

She felt herself pulled against the hard contours of Luke's body, his arm across her back, his hand resting possessively just below her breast. 'Sophie was fighting the inevitable yesterday,' he told the younger man. 'We had argued and she hit out at me by running to you.'

'Oh?' Nicholas was red with embarrassment. 'But this is all rather sudden, isn't it?'

'It sometimes happens like that,' Luke replied stiffly, and Sophie could feel the anger in his taut body. 'Your mother and father are expecting us back for breakfast,' he informed her, still in that stilted voice.

'Oh yes,' Nicholas realised he had been dismissed and remounted his horse. 'I should be getting back myself.'

'Oh, but——'

'Let him go, Sophie!' Luke said grimly.

She glanced up again and again to his dark forbidding face as they walked back to the house. His arm had fallen away from her waist as soon as they were out of sight of Nicholas, his mouth a thin angry line.

'You will never do that again,' he finally snapped, his eyes hard with anger.

She gave him a nervous look. 'Do what again?'

'Arrange to meet another man,' he bit out forcefully. 'I will not permit it. If I have to prove to you once again that you are mine then I will do so here and now.' He held her against the hardness of his body, bruising her soft flesh with his deliberate cruelty. His mouth clamped down on hers with one thought in mind, to punish her. His face was triumphant as he looked down at her, conscious of her response to him even in his anger. 'You are mine,' he told her arrogantly.

'I don't belong to anyone!' She fought to regain some of her old defiance.

His mouth twisted with cruel humour, openly taunting her. 'You will belong to me.'

'But I don't at the moment.' She pushed against his chest to release herself, able to breathe easier when she was apart from the seduction of his body.

'That does not mean you can arrange to meet another man as soon as my back is turned. I would take you now if I thought your rebellious nature would drive you into giving yourself to another man before we are married.'

'You're an arrogant swine! I did not arrange to meet

Nicholas, we met quite by accident. And how do you know I haven't already taken a lover? You said yourself that I enjoyed the pleasure I can get from my body.'

'But it will be pleasure only I give you.'

'Are you sure?' she taunted.

One of his hands spanned the slender width of her wrist, making her gasp with pain. 'Have you ever had a lover?'

He seemed more foreign in his anger and he frightened her a little. He usually treated her with amused tolerance, letting her taunts wash over him, but his attitude had changed to one of possession, of ownership.

'You're hurting me, Luke!' she cried, trying without success to remove his hand.

'Did you not know that pain can sometimes be as pleasurable as making love?' he scorned.

She bit her bottom lip to stop from crying out. 'Not this sort of pain. Please, Luke, let me go!'

'Ah—please,' his grip relaxed slightly. 'You plead very prettily. Have you taken a lover, Sophie?' he repeated abruptly. 'And I want the truth. I will know soon enough, anyway,' he added with taunting anticipation.

She coloured at his implication, shaking off his hand completely. 'Then it will give you something to think about.' She walked off towards the house, the short distance suddenly seeming much longer as she tried not to break into a run.

Luke swung her round. 'You will answer me!'

Her eyes flashed deeply violet. 'Why should I?' she challenged.

'Will you come to me a virgin?' he demanded.

'Will you?'

'Do not be ridiculous!'

'Oh, I see,' she scorned. 'It's all right for you to have been with other women, but I'm not allowed the same privilege as far as other men are concerned.'

'That was not what I meant.'

'Then what did you mean? That your experience was necessary? That you *had* to be the lover of all those women?'

'There have not been as many as the press reported.' His mouth twisted.

'If only half the stories were true you've had enough to form a harem!'

He scowled. 'I am thirty-eight and I have a normal appetite for sex, nothing more.'

'But I'm not allowed the same appetite?'

'Not before marriage.'

Sophie shook her head. 'The way you and men like you go through the female population you're expecting a lot, to expect to marry a virgin!'

'But I will be, will I not?' His taunting humour was back.

She flicked her hair back with childish defiance. 'Wait and see.'

This time he didn't attempt to stop her, but the sound of his throaty chuckle followed her. Her parents were already in the dining-room when she entered through the open patio doors. She avoided the sharp angry glance of her stepmother and went over to kiss her father on the cheek.

'Good morning, poppet,' he said gruffly. 'Luke,' he nodded to the younger man.

Sophie turned to see Luke standing behind her. She hadn't realised he had followed her into the house.

'Simon, Rosemary.' He held a chair back for Sophie to sit down. 'We were out for an early morning stroll.'

Sophie's lips clamped together. He was giving them the impression that they had arranged to go out together. He was adept at turning circumstances to his advantage, something she would have to remember in future.

'Coffee?' her stepmother asked him sharply.

'Thank you,' he nodded acceptance. 'Sophie and I have been discussing the wedding,' he spoke to her father.

Rosemary almost dropped the coffee-pot, she was shaking so much, whether with anger or some other emotion Sophie couldn't tell. 'Surely it's a bit soon to be discussing that? There's no hurry, is there?' she asked shrilly.

Sophie didn't think there was either. The longer she delayed being his wife the better. When he had free licence with her body she would become his slave in bed whenever he wanted her; she just couldn't fight the physical attraction between them.

'No hurry,' Luke agreed smoothly. 'Although I do not think we should wait too long.'

'I have to get used to the idea of losing my daughter,' Simon smiled. 'I don't want to lose her too soon.'

'I understand your sentiments,' Luke sipped the coffee. 'But I did explain last night that Sophie and I had been— impetuous. I would not like any repercussions from that impetuosity to put in an appearance before we have been legally bound together.'

Her father paled. 'You mean——'

'I mean it is highly likely that Sophie is carrying my child.'

'Oh!' Sophie's grasp was cut short by the pressure exerted on her knee by Luke's long fingers. She gulped back the rest of her protest, as those fingers pressed painfully into her skin.

'I see.' Her father didn't look as if he could take many more blows like this. 'That's something that hadn't occurred to me,' he said dully.

'No, and I am sorry to mention it. But you do understand . . .'

'Oh yes, we understand,' Rosemary said sarcastically. 'Sophie could be pregnant, so you're doing the decent thing and marrying her.'

'Rosemary!' her husband's shocked voice reprimanded.

Luke gave her a cool look. 'I did not say that.'

No, he hadn't said that, but he hadn't exactly denied it either! Sophie was fuming. It was bad enough that he had given her parents a completely erroneous impression without making things worse.

Her stepmother shrugged. 'It's fairly obvious what's happened. Sophie became infatuated with you and forced you into a situation no man could resist. That doesn't mean you have to marry her.'

'Rosemary!' her husband exclaimed sharply.

'Well, it's true, Simon. Sophie——'

'I was not an unwilling participant,' Luke cut in coldly.

'Rosemary, please,' her husband said wearily. 'They want to get married, and it seems it would be better if it were sooner rather than later. We'll make all the arrangements from here, Luke. I want my daughter to have the perfect wedding.'

Sophie could have cried at the raw pain in her father's voice—and she could cheerfully have slapped Luke's arrogant face for him. With everything he said he made things sound worse. To say she could be expecting his child!

To her shame she felt an inner glow at the thought of bearing his child. Would they have children? It gave the idea of her marriage to Luke a permanence she hadn't thought of. But of course a child could be a possibility between them, although she didn't think Luke would let that happen as easily as he was letting her parents believe.

Luke seemed to feel no remorse when she attacked him with it later, the two of them in the room that had been converted into a studio, supposedly to work on the portrait for her father's birthday.

He shrugged off her attack. 'What difference does it make? Besides, the decision has been made and I see no reason to delay carrying it out. I do not intend to spend months as a fiancé when all I want is to get you into my bed.'

'It didn't occur to you that you've deeply shocked my father with your lies?' Her eyes sparkled angrily.

'He is a man of the world, he would know how easy it is to be carried away by the more basic emotions, so carried away that we did not think of taking the necessary steps to prevent the possibility of a child.'

'But we haven't done anything like that!' She could almost have stamped her foot with frustration.

'You have only to say the word . . .' he said meaningly.

'You know very well what I mean,' she snapped. 'That painting has put us in a position where we have to marry each other, but do you——'

'I do not *have* to marry anyone.'

'Do you have to make things sound worse than they are?' she carried on talking as if he hadn't spoken. 'Implying that I could be pregnant!'

'But you could be, in thought if not in deed.'

She blushed, the knowledge that he thought of making love to her strangely exhilarating. 'But I'm not! And I'm sure my father didn't need that added shock.'

'And your stepmother? How do you think she feels?'

'She hasn't spoken to me about it.' But no doubt she would, choosing her moment carefully!

'Neither has your father, but you profess to know his feelings on the matter.' Luke came over and straightened the angle of her jaw before going back to his easel. 'I realise it is hard for a father to accept that his little girl is a woman, but I do not intend waiting for you while your father comes to terms with the fact. I desire you, and I want you in my bed as soon as possible.'

'Luke!' Her face was scarlet with embarrassment.

He put down his paintbrush, his mouth quirking with amusement. 'Why should I lie? You have been destined for my bed since we first met.'

'Since I went over the handlebars of my bicycle with such elegance?' she teased with brittle humour.

He nodded. 'Since then. I tried very hard to get you to give me your address, but you proved obstinate in not telling me.'

'That was because——'

'Because you knew we would meet later, because you intended making a fool of me.'

She looked at him beneath lowered lashes. 'And did I?'

'I do not think so.' He grinned. 'Am I not getting what I wanted all along.'

She raised her eyebrows. 'To marry me?'

He smiled, suddenly looking much younger and less forbidding. 'You in my bed,' he corrected, coming over to the sofa where she sat. He cupped her chin, forcing her to look into his velvet brown eyes. 'I will be a very jealous lover,' he warned her softly. 'But I will be a generous one.'

'I don't want your money,' she protested.

His long sensitive fingers played with her parted lips. 'I was not talking about money,' he said huskily.

'Oh.' She couldn't meet the look in his eyes.

Luke laughed throatily. 'It is good to see you can still blush.'

'And why shouldn't I?' she challenged crossly. 'I'm not the one with experience.'

He frowned, suddenly serious. 'Does it really bother you that much that there have been other women?'

'Yes! No! I don't know. I—men are usually the experienced ones, aren't they.'

'Usually,' he agreed. 'And I really have no way of erasing my past. But I want you to know that not one of those women meant more to me than a brief affair. I can say no more.'

'How do I know I'll mean any more?'

'You cannot know,' he answered truthfully. 'But I have never married before, that should tell you something.'

'It tells me you must want me pretty badly,' she said softly.

'Insanely so,' Luke acknowledged huskily. 'I have since the moment I saw your hair like sunlight and your eyes like violets. You have the power to drive a man wild with wanting you, and you will be mine.'

'Yours . . .' She felt mesmerised by the seduction in his voice.

'Yes, *mine*.' His head bent and he claimed her mouth in a searching kiss, gently prising her lips apart with the tip of his tongue.

She welcomed the throbbing urgency of his body against her, her hands unbuttoning his shirt to touch the smooth skin beneath. His mouth moved the long length of her throat, his warm breath caressing her skin.

Luke leant back to look at her, his hands moving to the buttons on her blouse, releasing each one with slow deliberation. He watched every expression on her face, lightly touching the tip of her hardened nipple as she gasped her pleasure.

Sophie shuddered with reaction, wanting to break away but unable to. She watched his dark head as his mouth closed about her breast, arousing her to further delight.

'Oh, Sophie,' he groaned. 'This is not the right time or place for this.'

She could feel him fighting to regain control, feel the tautness of his thighs, the raggedness of his breathing, and although he protested he made no effort to stop kissing her. 'Luke, you—you will be patient with me when we're— when we're married?' she asked breathlessly.

He was still touching her breasts, enjoying her pleasure as much as his own. 'Patient with you?' he asked vaguely.

She licked her lips. 'With my inexperience.'

He drew a deep shuddering breath and moved back to rebutton her blouse for her. 'I will try. But you tempt me until I can think of nothing but you beneath me as I make love to you. I am going to be a very demanding husband.'

She didn't think she was going to mind that. Right now she didn't think she was going to mind that at all.

Luke stood up, buttoning his own shirt with shaking fingers. 'I think you should go now, Sophie. With you my control does not seem to last very long.'

She swung her legs to the floor and stood up unsteadily. 'But the portrait . . .'

He smiled. 'I have a feeling it will not be completed until we have been married for some time, until I can look at you and not want to make love to you.'

She smoothed her skirt down to cover her embarrassment, sure that no Englishman would talk so bluntly about desire and lovemaking. But then she wasn't marrying an Englishman. 'You managed to almost finish the other one,' she reminded him.

His brown eyes teased her. 'I was driven on to do that one to the exclusion of all else. But I will not need to look at it for much longer, soon I will have the real thing.'

To think of Luke looking at that painting whenever he was alone, desiring her, made her cheeks burn. 'How soon, Luke?'

'Very soon if I have my way, *cara*. Please go now. You understand?' he asked gently.

She understood, leaving the room as he requested. Not that she thought she would have had the same resolve if they had been alone at his apartment. Everyone believed them to be lovers and so she saw no harm in it becoming a reality, would welcome it even. Anything to stop this constant let-down feeling when their lovemaking wasn't consummated.

Her stepmother was alone in the lounge when she got

downstairs, making her wish she had checked before entering. Rosemary's barbs were the last thing she needed right now, with her lips and body still tingling from Luke's caresses.

'My God, you look a mess,' was her stepmother's opening comment. 'I don't need to ask what you've been doing.'

Sophie moved to look out of the window. 'Where's Daddy?'

'In his study,' her stepmother answered shortly. 'I suppose you think you've been very clever, trapping a man like Luke into marriage.'

'I didn't——'

'Didn't you?' Rosemary's voice rose shrilly, her blue eyes venomous. 'Well, don't think a little thing like your marriage will put a stop to Luke and me meeting. What we have is very special, you see, so special that Luke wouldn't even discuss it with you. When he's become tired of you our relationship will still be just as intense. He's had girls like you before, they mean nothing.'

Sophie was white. 'You forget one thing, he's *marrying* me.'

Rosemary smiled. 'Only to placate your father. Things could become very awkward for Luke if it was known he had an affair with you—your father is an influential man. After all, I could hardly marry him myself, now could I? No, I think it's much better this way, keep it in the family, so to speak.'

'You can't mean that!' Sophie was incredulous.

'You just wait and see. I'll still have Luke long after he's tired of your innocence and naïveté.'

'I—I think I'll go to my room.' Sophie felt sick.

'You do that,' her stepmother said with a satisfied smile. 'But remember one thing, Luke is mine—and he'll stay mine long after he's forgotten you.'

CHAPTER SIX

IT was the society wedding of the year—everyone said so, from the media to the two hundred selected guests. It caused quite a stir, the announcement of the marriage between the daughter of Simon and Rosemary Bedford to the celebrated artist Luke Vittorio.

Sophie had been horrified at the amount of publicity they had attracted, and found herself followed by the press wherever she went. Luke seemed immune to their followers, taking it all in his stride. But then he was used to living his life in the public eye, something she would have to accept as his wife.

Because of Luke's insistence the wedding had taken place only six weeks after it had first been put to her father, the rush and bustle of the last few weeks making it almost impossible for them to spend any time alone. Consequently Sophie now felt herself married to a stranger, almost faltering as she had seen the look of arrogant possession on Luke's face as she walked down the aisle on her father's arm.

The reception seemed no less frightening, the congratulations and kisses all receiving a plastic smile in return that seemed frozen on her lips. Luke's long fingers rested lightly on her elbow, although she had no doubt they would clamp on like steel tentacles if she attempted to move from his side. They hadn't spoken to each other at all, her nervousness increasing as the time for them to leave came closer and closer.

'I believe it is time you went and changed,' Luke spoke to her. 'We have to leave shortly.'

She had to stop herself making a mad dash for the house; the reception was being held in a marquee in the garden. 'I—Yes, I—I'll go now.'

Deep brown eyes looked down at her white frightened face. 'Would you like me to come with you?'

Her face coloured scarlet. 'No! No, I—I think I can manage.'

His firm mouth twisted into a smile. 'I was not offering to help you change, merely undress.'

She knew that—oh yes, she knew that. But his desire frightened her too, as everything about this marriage did. As from today she would be completely under Luke's dominance, a prisoner of her own desire for the hardness of his body and the temptation of his mouth.

'I won't be long.' She moved quickly away from his side to go to her bedroom.

Her two suitcases stood just inside the door ready for their departure, the rest of her things already moved into Luke's apartment in London. She slumped down on the bed, taking a last look round the room. She had slept here for the last time; she and Luke would be given a room with a double bed when they visited.

She looked up with a feeling of apprehension as her stepmother came into the room, beautifully turned out in a sapphire blue silk suit and matching Juliet cap. She looked young enough to be the bride herself, and Sophie had seen Luke watching her as she moved among the guests, his expression telling her nothing of his thoughts.

'Why are you just sitting there?' Rosemary demanded, opening the wardrobe doors to take out the purple dress Sophie had chosen as her going-away outfit. They were flying straight to Paris for the week, so the dress had been chosen for travelling in as well as for its attractiveness. 'Shouldn't you be changing?'

Sophie stood up, moving with dragging steps, unzipping the flowing white wedding gown and stepping out of it as if in a dream. She took off the long veil, releasing her hair from its confining curls to flow smoothly down her back.

Her stepmother tutted impatiently. 'Do hurry up, Sophie. Everyone is waiting for you downstairs.'

Including Luke! Oh God, she felt so nervous. He was her *husband* now, she was Sophie Vittorio, his wife.

Rosemary looked at her closely. 'You aren't going to be sick, are you?'

She had hardly finished speaking before Sophie made a mad dash to the bathroom, the champagne and small amount of food she had attempted to force down her soon leaving her body with much more rapidity than she had eaten them. She emerged from the bathroom pale-faced and drawn, the sickness still with her.

'So you're pregnant after all,' Rosemary said dryly.

Sophie's eyes widened with shock. 'I am not,' she protested. 'It was just too much champagne on an empty stomach.'

'No need to lie to me, Sophie. I know the truth, remember?'

The truth as Luke had led them to believe! 'I am not pregnant!'

'I'm not stupid.' Rosemary hung the white wedding gown in the wardrobe. 'I don't suppose you should really have worn this colour—in the circumstances,' she said thoughtfully.

'There are no circumstances! And if all the girls who should wear white wore it the colour would go out of fashion tomorrow.'

'Mm, that's true. Still, I must say you fell pregnant

pretty easily. Of course Luke's a virile man, but even so . . .'

'*I am not pregnant!*' Sophie's words were forced out between gritted teeth as she strove to hold on to her temper.

'Of course you are. I noticed our little friend didn't call on you this month.'

'I——' Sophie's words of denial remained unspoken. What was the use? Rosemary would never believe that the tension and nervousness of the last few weeks were the cause of her body not functioning as it should. There could certainly be no other reason for it! 'Only time will tell,' she amended.

'It certainly will. Your father will be delighted—now that he's got over his initial surprise. Not that *I* blame you, I know how persuasive Luke can be.'

'I know,' Sophie said through stiff lips.

Rosemary gave a husky laugh. 'No need to be jealous, Sophie. After all, he'll be your husband.'

'And what does that prove?'

Her stepmother looked thoughtful. 'You're right,' she said finally. 'It doesn't prove a thing.'

'That's what I thought.' Sophie turned on her heel. 'Excuse me, I have to wash.'

'I'll wait for you and help you change.'

Sophie didn't protest, escaping to the privacy of the bathroom. She hadn't needed her stepmother to tell her that her marriage wasn't worth the paper it was written on, that the marriage vows meant nothing to Luke, even if he had spoken them beautifully. It had been difficult not to believe he meant every word, the seriousness and sincerity of his voice was totally convincing. But she knew it was all an act, a lie.

The smile was fixed back on her lips by the time she walked down the long staircase, bathed in the admiration of the guests. There was a deep approving look in the eyes of her bridegroom, but she couldn't be sure if that was for her or for her stepmother walking two steps behind her. She had a feeling it was the latter.

Their goodbyes were full of laughter and teasing advice, the single hug from her father making a huge lump rise in her throat. They had said their goodbyes before the ceremony, but it was still a wrench, her final step from being a girl to a woman, no longer just her father's daughter but another man's wife.

Luke looked at her in the confines of the car. 'Ready?'

Would she ever be ready for the life she had allowed herself to be trapped into? She doubted it. 'Ready,' she nodded.

Rosemary appeared at the open car window. 'Be gentle with her, Luke,' she advised.

'I intend to be,' he replied softly.

'But *especially* gentle,' she said with relish. 'It's a dangerous time, you know.'

Luke frowned at her innuendo. 'What is?'

'Oh dear, Sophie hasn't told you yet?'

'Told me what?'

She gave a satisfied smile. 'I'll leave it to your little bride to tell you. Have fun!' She stepped back from the car, waving with the other guests.

The car shot away so fast that Sophie was flung back against the headrest. 'What did she mean?' Luke asked grimly.

She turned slowly from waving to look apprehensively at his cold hard face. 'I don't know,' she lied miserably.

His foot pressed firmly down on the accelerator. 'Yes, you do. What was she talking about, Sophie?'

'It's all your fault,' she accused shakily. 'You gave them the idea in the first place.'

'Explain yourself,' he snapped.

She took a deep breath, her hands entwined nervously on her lap. 'My stepmother has the mistaken idea that I'm expecting your baby,' she told him.

Luke gave her a hard probing look, noting the vulnerability of her trembling mouth, the shadows in her eyes. 'And why should she think that?'

'Because you told them——'

'But why does she think it is a fact?' he asked abruptly.

'Because I—I was sick just now and I—I haven't—I——'

'I see,' cold angry eyes raked over her slender curves. 'And is it true?'

'You know it isn't!' she gasped. 'We haven't——'

'The child does not have to be mine,' he interrupted abruptly.

Sophie gave him a horrified stare. 'You can't be serious!'

'I am very serious. If I find you have . . . The marriage will end immediately if I find it to be true,' he said harshly.

'But you know it isn't,' she said desperately, tears swimming in her eyes.

'The evidence would seem to show otherwise.'

'Evidence!' Anger entered her voice. 'I'm not on trial, Luke. Just because I happen not to have—well, that doesn't mean anything other than that I've had a lot on my mind lately. It sometimes has that effect.'

'I hope for your sake that that is the case. I would not like to think that your afternoon meeting with Sedgwick-Jones came to any more than a tumble in the hay.'

'A tumble in the . . . You're disgusting!'

'I am your husband,' he stated, one of his hands moving out to clasp her chin in a cruel grasp. The expression in his eyes could only be called possessive. 'You will do well to remember that it is I and I alone who have the right to claim your body.'

Sophie wrenched out of his grasp, uncaring of the pain it

caused. 'And when that happens you'll know once and for all that I'm not pregnant.'

'How will I know that?'

'Isn't it obvious?' she snapped.

He gave her another cold look. 'We shall see.'

Sophie was treated to his icy politeness all the way to the airport, accepting the magazines he bought her as an indication that they were not to talk on the short flight either. She was right; Luke sat back in his seat, his eyes closed.

Instead of reading the magazines as he had obviously intended her to do she looked at him, wishing she were indeed off on the ecstatic honeymoon everyone believed them to be. She had seen the air hostess giving Luke covetous looks, her disappointment obvious as she saw the confetti in Sophie's hair.

Sophie could understand the girl's interest in Luke, he did look rather magnificent today. He was dressed in an iron-grey suit, his linen immaculate. Of course he was very attractive anyway, but today he looked even more so, very sexy, his dark good looks magnetic.

It was dinner time when they arrived at their hotel, their rooms adjoining the large bathroom they were to share. Sophie heaved a sigh of relief when she saw they had separate rooms; at least she would be able to change her clothing in privacy. It was strange just how shy she felt, a sense of the occasion always with her.

'Your room is satisfactory?' Luke asked her once they were alone.

Magnificent was more the word she would have used to describe it, the decor was deliberately old-fashioned and gracious. 'It's lovely, thank you.'

He nodded distantly as if he had never been in any doubt of her answer. 'You wish dinner to be sent up or shall we go down to the dining-room?'

'The dining-room, I think,' came her swift reply, choosing the lesser of two evils. She didn't want to be up here alone with him any sooner than she needed to be.

Luke smiled as if reading her thoughts. 'You can use the bathroom first,' and he went through to his own room.

Sophie hurriedly did as he said, not wishing to be still under the shower when he himself decided to use the bathroom. She was just putting the final touches to her lipstick when Luke came through to her room, devastatingly attractive in a fitted brown suit and tan shirt. She herself was wearing one of the evening dresses bought specifically for her honeymoon, its golden colour matching her hair perfectly. It fitted like a second skin over her curves before flowing down to her ankles, her height added to by slender gold sandals.

Luke make no comment about her appearance, but took out a long jewellery case from his pocket. 'Turn around,' he ordered her.

She felt the coolness of the gold against her skin, watching their reflections in the mirror as Luke fastened a chunky gold choker about her throat. 'It's—it's very beautiful.' She touched it wonderingly, surprised by his gift.

Luke's hands remained possessively on her shoulders; he looked at her in the mirror as his lips followed the path of the choker. 'It could not hope to match your own beauty,' he said throatily.

Sophie's breath caught in her throat and she felt herself tremble as he pulled her back against him, his thighs hard against her. 'You—you're very flattering.'

He moved away from her, straightening his cuff as if their closeness had never happened. He certainly showed none of the breathless excitement that she felt. 'One does not flatter one's wife,' he told her. 'One merely comments on her appearance—and you look beautiful.'

'Thank you.' His explanation took away any intimacy

that might have been between them. 'Shall we go down now?'

'Of course,' he nodded.

The dining-room adjoined the ballroom, making it possible for Sophie to listen to the romantic music drifting in from there and watch the dancers rather than sit selfconsciously aware of the friction between herself and Luke.

The meal was excellent, as was the service, but then that was to be expected with a celebrity like Luke Vittorio staying at the hotel. Sophie felt out of her depth and consequently felt too shy to answer Luke's occasional remarks with anything more than monosyllables.

Having come down late for their meal they were among the last to leave the dining-room. Sophie felt her panic returning with the end of their meal, tired but knowing that sleep would not be something Luke had in mind for their return to their suite.

She clutched at his sleeve as they left the dining-room. 'Could we—er—could we go in and dance?' She looked at him hopefully, dreading the night ahead of her because it would make her completely Luke's. Anything to delay that moment.

Luke's expression wasn't forthcoming. 'It is late, and you have had a long day.'

She gave him a bright smile meant to show him she was wide awake. 'I'd like to dance, Luke,' she asked pleadingly.

'I really think——'

'Oh, please, Luke,' she pouted prettily. 'It's early yet. Why, it isn't even eleven o'clock yet.'

'I did have other plans for this evening.' His eyes were deeply brown as he looked down at her.

She blushed. 'But we could dance a little first.'

'First . . .?'

'Before we go up to our rooms.' Her colour stayed high at his mockery.

'Very well,' he at last agreed.

Sophie could have sighed her relief as they were shown to a table, accepting the champagne Luke ordered for them.

'To us,' he toasted softly.

'Yes,' she agreed breathlessly, finding the look in his eyes more and more seductive. He shouldn't be looking at her like that, not in front of all these people. She gulped down the champagne, gasping as the bubbles went up her nose. She put her glass out to Luke to be refilled.

He did so, his mouth quirking into a smile. 'I hope you do not intend getting yourself drunk,' he said teasingly.

'And incapable?' she joked, her eyes twinkling from the effect of the alcohol.

'Especially incapable.'

'I'll try not to,' she couldn't look at him.

'Would you like to dance now?'

Did she want to be that close to him? 'I—well, I——'

'That is what we came in here for after all,' he reminded her.

She stood up jerkily. 'Yes, yes, I suppose it is.'

'You do not sound too sure.'

She gave him that bright smile again. 'Of course I'm sure.' She just wasn't sure about being in his arms.

He danced well, as she had known he would, and by the looks they were receiving from the guests at the hotel he was also being recognised. The people were too polite to actually come over and speak to him but it made Sophie feel very conspicuous.

'Forget them,' Luke whispered against her earlobe, his lips caressing her creamy skin.

Sophie jerked in his arms, just the touch of his mouth unnerving her. Oh God, what was she going to be like when they went upstairs together! 'Them?' she asked huskily.

'Forget other people.' He pulled her gently against him, closing the gap between them.

All Sophie's breath seemed to leave her body at his closeness. 'I—It's rather difficult when they keep staring at us.'

'Changed your mind about going to our suite?'

His lips on her throat made her burn all over, her breathing constricted. 'No!' she said sharply. 'No, I still want to dance.' She tried to get normality back in her voice and failed.

Luke shrugged. 'I am in no hurry.'

She was sure he wasn't. After all, he had all week to make her his wife in the fullest sense, he had no need to rush it. He knew there was no escape for her.

They danced together for over an hour, by which time the champagne had begun to give her a much less frightening impression of her husband. The tension left her body and the two of them danced slowly together, often not bothering to move to the music as it changed tempo. Sophie's head rested on Luke's shoulder, her arms up about his neck.

'Enough is enough, Sophie,' he said suddenly. 'It is time to go to our suite.'

That brought her back down to reality, and she looked up at him. 'Do we have to?'

There was a certain tautness about the sensuality of his mouth. 'Unless you wish for me to make love to you right here,' he said grimly.

'Oh!'

'So, we leave?'

'Yes,' she nodded hurriedly. She had pushed him too far already, she couldn't hope to push her luck any further.

They went up alone in the lift, the tension between them a tangible thing. Luke was watching her with brooding eyes and she could be in no doubt of his desire for her. But then what else could she expect?—that was the reason he had married her.

The nightgown bought for her wedding night seemed hardly worth the bother of putting it on once she looked at herself in the mirror. She had turned the lights down to a golden glow, but still her body was visible through its transparency. She hadn't realised it was quite so revealing, her every curve revealed, her breasts uptilted and inviting.

The door to her balcony stood open, enticing her to gaze out at the sight of Paris by moonlight. It seemed that it was all spread out before her, curiously quiet up here, and very, very beautiful. It was a view for lovers, and Sophie shivered as she felt Luke's arms go about her waist, his hands coming to rest on the flatness of her stomach as he pulled her back against the hardness of his body.

'You are not cold?' he murmured against her throat.

She was burning! 'No.'

'Beautiful, is it not?' But she had the idea he wasn't talking about Paris.

'Very,' she felt tongue-tied by the movement of his hands on her body as they moved up to cup her breasts, his fingers caressing.

'Shall we go inside?' he invited. 'You must be a little chilled.'

'No, I——'

'I am not going to hurt you,' he said gently, taking her hand and leading her back inside.

He was dressed as he had been the night she and her stepmother had invaded the privacy of his bedroom, the white towelling robe that reached down to his knees the only article of clothing he wore. His hair was still damp from the shower he had just taken, the smell of his after-shave tangy and stirring to the senses.

He retained his hold on her hand as she would have moved away, his gaze resting intimately on her almost naked body. 'I have waited a long time for this,' he murmured. 'Only the painting has kept me sane the last few weeks.'

Her eyes widened. 'You still have it?'

Luke smiled. 'But of course. I have said you do not have to see it, but that does not mean I cannot look at it from time to time. It shows you as I would like to see you all the time, wanton from lovemaking—*my* lovemaking,' he added hardly.

She knew his anger had returned by the assessing look in his eyes, knew he was thinking of her stepmother's broad hints as to her non-existent condition, knew he would not be appeased until he had possessed her for himself and learnt the truth.

'I have said I will be a generous lover,' he continued harshly. 'But at this moment I do not know if I can keep that promise. I have to know, you see, Sophie. I have to know!'

'Please be gentle with me, Luke.'

'For the reason Rosemary implied?' he demanded bitterly.

'No! I——'

'Do not make any more denials,' he ordered. 'I do not want to hear them. You are my wife, this is our wedding night, and I do not intend to let you be haunted by the lovemaking of another man.'

'Another man . , .?'

'Sedgwick-Jones,' he said harshly. 'But by the time I have finished with you you will think of no man but me.'

'I—— '

'No more protests,' he swung her up into his arms. 'Think of no one but me.'

How could she possibly think of anyone but him, with him pinning her to the bed with his body, his hands touching and caressing her, his mouth in total possession of her?

His onslaught to her senses was slow and deliberate, allowing her no chance to be anything but totally aroused by him, her arms encircling his waist as she felt herself sinking into the total oblivion of his seduction.

'Untie my robe,' he ordered her roughly. 'I want to be naked against you.'

Sophie wanted it too, wanted it desperately. He was playing with her body like an expert, arousing her and enjoying her arousal. She did as he asked, slipping his robe off his shoulders. She felt shy about looking at him, the perfection of a man's body was a revelation to her, the ripple of muscle over shoulders and stomach, the dark hair completely covering his body, just the male beauty of him.

She no longer felt embarrassed, but touched him in wonderment, his sharply indrawn breath all she needed to show her how her touch affected him. He was no longer the aggressor, lying back to let her take the initiative, his eyes half-closed in pleasure, his breathing ragged and laboured.

Her hands passed with wonder over the strength of his chest, the flatness of his stomach, her butterfly movements hesitating about further intimacies.

'Please continue,' Luke invited huskily.

She couldn't now he had told her to, and her brief exploration came to an abrupt end, her face scarlet. She looked at him helplessly, her newfound confidence deserting her.

Luke sat up, leaning on one elbow to look down at her. 'Let me take off this ridiculous trifle,' he caressed her body through the thinness of her gown. 'I want to be closer to you.'

Her husky laugh caught in her throat. 'We can't be much closer!'

'Oh yes, we can.' The nightgown was quickly dispensed with and he set about showing her just how much closer they could be.

Sophie's relative inexperience didn't seem to trouble Luke as he took her to the very edge of a sensual abyss. And then he took her over, well over, her one feeling of pain soon forgotten as a feeling of exquisite joy invaded every pore of her body. That Luke knew of her pleasure she had no doubt, conscious of a more urgent thrusting of his own body as he brought them both to trembling fulfilment, his body weightless above her.

They lay exhausted in each other's arms, their naked bodies still joined. Sophie had never known such pleasure, never felt she completely belonged to anyone before. And she hadn't. None of the tentative kisses she had received from Nicholas and boys like him compared to anything like the complete devastation she had just passed through with Luke.

His arms clamped about her as she stirred against him. 'Be still,' he commanded. 'You are not to leave me.'

'I wasn't going to.' She snuggled against him.

'Good.' He held her against him and she felt the desire ebbing back into his body. 'The night is far from over.'

And it was. Luke took her once more in the night, as before raising her to the heights so that she was clinging and weak in his arms. But not once did any words of tenderness or love pass his lips, his only interest seeming to be in her body and the pleasure he could extract from it.

But by the time she woke in his arms late in the morning she knew herself to be deeply in love with her husband, had half known it before their marriage, but now knew it with a certainty that would never pass. She was married to the one man she would ever love, and she had no way of knowing how he really felt about her.

She slipped out of the bed, pulling on Luke's towelling robe to wander out on to the balcony. Paris was still as beautiful by day, although not as seducing. She knew she had pleased Luke physically, had known he found her response to him exciting, but she had no way of knowing how long that was going to last.

She melted back against him as she felt his arms go about her from behind. She rubbed her head against his chin. 'I thought you were asleep,' she turned to smile at him.

'When you are not beside me?' He kissed her throat. 'Come back to bed, Mrs Vittorio,' he ordered huskily.

'Certainly not!' she laughed softly. 'It's very late in the morning, and we haven't even had breakfast yet.'

'I was just about to partake of mine—you.'

She twisted out of his arms, finding she could still blush as she saw his nakedness. Of course, she was wearing his bathrobe! 'I think you've had me enough for one day.'

He shook his head. 'I have not had you at all today—last night was a different matter.'

She looked at him shyly. 'But aren't you exhausted?'

'From making love to you? Never. Are you?'

Strangely enough she wasn't, feeling refreshed by the physical love he had shown her at least. She shook her head wordlessly.

Luke opened his arms to her. 'Then come to me, Sophie. If you must think of mundane things like food we will have lunch later—much later.'

She burrowed against him. 'I'm not really hungry either.'

'I did not say I was not hungry,' he growled. 'But my hunger is of a different kind.'

'You're insatiable,' she blushed.

'Yes,' he agreed willingly.

It had gone one o'clock when they finally called down for lunch. Sophie felt sure the waiter was looking at them knowingly as he served their meal to them on the balcony, although she knew there was no evidence of the night they had just spent in the now tidied order of her bedroom. Luke

looked as confident as ever, ignoring the waiter and seeming to have eyes only for her.

'Oh, Luke!' she coloured delicately once they were
alone. 'I'm sure he knew.'

Luke sipped his wine. 'Knew what, *cara*?'

'That we—that we had——'

'Just got out of bed,' he finished teasingly. 'But we have.'

'I know. But—well, I—It——'

'Do not blush so, Sophie. It is normal to be this way on
one's honeymoon.'

'Yes, but——'

'You are too sensitive. Paris was made for love.'

For love, yes, but did they have love? She very much
doubted it. If their fevered lovemaking of last night had not
brought any words of love from him then she didn't think
anything else ever would. She was an attractive female to
him, someone he desired, and the fact that she was his wife
simply gave him access to her any time he chose.

Right now, after the night and morning they had just
shared, she should be basking in Luke's love, instead of
which she was still uncertain of him in every way. Physical
pleasure couldn't hope to replace the love she craved, no
matter how satisfying it could be.

'Do not look so worried, Sophie,' Luke said lightly. 'No
one is going to reprimand you for spending the morning in
bed with your husband.'

'It's just so embarrassing that everyone should *know*.'

'They would know anyway.' He fed her a grape from the
bowl in the middle of the table. 'You have that certain look
about you.'

'The look of your possession.'

'If you like, yes.'

Oh, she liked—she liked his possession of her too much
for her peace of mind. It was as she had known it would be,

she felt fired by his every touch, while he gave every indication of being able to control his desire for her, was able to control it and master it if necessary. Never once during their lovemaking had he given in to his own passion until he was sure she had found satisfaction, never once losing control as completely as she had.

'Do you believe me now?' she asked shyly.

'About what, *cara*?'

'About—about Nicholas, about this mythical baby.'

'Ah, yes. You were telling the truth, you could not be carrying anyone's child before yesterday. You were untouched.'

'And if I hadn't been—untouched, I mean? If you couldn't be convinced that way that there was no baby?'

'Time would have shown one way or the other.'

'Yes, but——'

'Why do you persist in these questions, Sophie? They are irrelevant.'

'Not to me.'

'Why?'

'Because it isn't. What would you have done if you had—if you had made love to me last night and found I had had other lovers?'

'I do not know.'

'Yes, you do. Tell me, Luke,' she pleaded.

'Very well,' he said impatiently. 'If that had been the case, in the light of what Rosemary disclosed yesterday, we would have returned to London today. I had already warned you I did not want a wife who had been with other men, especially a wife who could be carrying another man's child. But I now know that is not true, so it does not apply.'

'I see,' she bit her lip. 'But our marriage would have ended?'

'Of course,' he said haughtily.

That was what she had thought. Luke would have con-

victed her on such flimsy evidence as an omission on the
part of nature and perhaps one misdemeanour in her dist-
ant past. The thought made her heart heavy.

'Drink your coffee, Sophie,' he encouraged, 'and then I
will take you sightseeing.'

She automatically did as he said, knowing that she was
here now only because she had never been tempted to give
herself to another man in the past. It wasn't a very comfort-
ing thought.

CHAPTER SEVEN

THEY spent ten idyllic days and nights in Paris, Luke
deciding to stay on an extra couple of days at the last
minute. Sophie had found it amazing at the time that the
hotel management had somehow managed to accommod-
ate them at short notice when they were turning other
people away. Luke's powerful influence, no doubt.

The honeymoon had been everything any girl could wish
for, although she really couldn't say she had seen much of
Paris itself. It had only taken a word or look from either of
them to spark the flame of desire that never seemed to be far
away for them to be back in bed together, their bodies
entwined.

The flight back to England had been short and unevent-
ful, but not filled with the cold reserve Luke had treated her
to on the flight out. They had talked together, laughed
together, and Sophie couldn't help wondering if she was
being silly to feel apprehensive about their return to every-
day life. After all, all honeymoon couples had to face the

same upheaval, the wondering if the honeymoon period was indeed over. And she did have one advantage over a lot of women; Luke worked at home, making it possible for her to see him at any time.

She looked up now as he walked unannounced into the bathroom as she took a shower to freshen her up after the flight, her initial shyness with him long forgotten in their continual lovemaking. She smiled at him through the spray from the shower, aware that he was saying something to her but unable to hear him above the noise of the falling water. She shook her head, shrugging her puzzlement.

She gasped as he stepped fully clothed into the shower beside her, her senses spinning as he took the soap from her unresisting fingers and began to soap her body all over. 'You're mad, Luke,' she laughed huskily. 'Your clothes— they're ruined!' The white shirt and trousers were in fact clinging to him like a second skin, his body seducing her through the wet material.

He discarded the soap and backed her up against the wall, her body moulded to his. 'You could not hear what I was saying.'

Sophie spluttered with laughter. 'But I would have been out of here in a moment.'

Luke switched off the running water, the urgency of his body communicating itself to her as they clung together. 'It would not have been soon enough for me,' he kissed her wet lips, licking the droplets of water from her face. 'I want you now,' he groaned, lifting her up into his arms and carrying her into the bedroom they were to share.

'But my parents, Luke,' she offered a token resistance as he lowered her on to the bed. 'They're expecting us for tea.'

He shrugged, stripping off his wet clothes. 'So we will arrive for dinner instead. I have not made love to you for over five hours.'

'Oh, Luke!' she laughed, raising her arms to him invitingly as he stood before her naked.

Hours later she stirred against him, not wanting to remind him of their promise to visit her parents but knowing they couldn't leave it any later to go.

Luke put a restraining hand on her thigh as she made a move to swing her legs to the floor. 'Where are you going?'

'We must go now, Luke.'

'Not yet.' He pulled her back into his arms, kissing her druggingly. 'We do not have to leave yet,' he moaned softly against her throat.

Sophie fought for some control over her senses, struggling to hold back the rising of her own desire. 'We must, Luke,' she insisted. 'Don't you ever tire of making love to me?'

'No,' his hand rested possessively on her breast.

'But we seem to have done nothing else since we married.'

His mouth tightened into a grim line, his eyes suddenly cold. He stood up. 'You are bored with my lovemaking,' he said abruptly.

'No! I——'

'Do not make matters any worse,' he snapped. 'I had forgotten that for the English the end of the honeymoon means the end of the more enjoyable part of physical love, that we must become more conventional, save our desire for the night hours.'

'Please, I didn't mean——'

He put up a hand to silence her. 'I will endeavour to show more control in future. Get dressed now and we will be on our way.'

She had angered him, she knew that, and he wouldn't give her a chance to explain herself. Far from being bored with his lovemaking she felt it was the only thing holding them together. If he took that away from her she would have nothing of him at all.

It was indeed dinner time when they reached her parents' house, and Martin showed them into the lounge where her father and Rosemary were waiting for them.

Sophie ran into her father's arms, suddenly his little girl again. 'I've missed you,' she said through a mist of tears.

Rosemary received her kiss on the cheek coolly. 'You aren't supposed to miss your father on your honeymoon,' she said dryly.

Sophie blushed at the rebuke, conscious of the censure in Luke's eyes too. She hadn't meant that remark the way it sounded, hadn't in fact been conscious of missing her father until this moment. 'I didn't mean——'

'She did not mean she had missed him that much,' Luke cut in tauntingly. 'I did not give her the time for that.'

'Yes, well . . .' her father cleared his throat noisily. 'We expected you earlier than this.'

Luke's deep brown eyes mocked her flushed face. 'Sophie was a little tired after our journey. I thought it better for her to—rest.'

A dark red hue appeared in her father's cheeks as he accurately read Luke's implication. 'I—er—Rosemary tells me that there could be a—a reason for Sophie to rest right now.'

Sophie was horrified. 'No! That isn't——'

'It is a possibility,' Luke interrupted calmly.

She gave him a sharp look. 'But we——'

'Especially now,' he continued smoothly.

She paled. She supposed it *was* a possibility, more than a possibility. A family had never been discussed by them and so consequently they had taken no precaution not to have one. How ironic if she should fall pregnant now, how very ironic!

'So you could be going to be a grandfather,' Rosemary taunted her husband.

'It would also make you a grandmother,' Sophie put in sweetly.

Rosemary gave her a look of irritation. 'Of course it wouldn't! A step-grandmother, perhaps . . .'

'No child could come out with a mouthful like that,' Luke said with humour.

'I'm glad you find the prospect of fatherhood so amusing,' Rosemary snapped. 'It would certainly make a difference to your life-style.'

He looked unperturbed by her outburst. 'Marriage has already done that.'

'I—er—I suggest we all go in to dinner,' Simon put in mildly.

Sophie was very quiet through dinner, Rosemary and Luke seeming to have got over their brief antagonism, her stepmother dazzling the two men with her charm and sparkling wit.

There was a certain coolness between herself and Luke as they prepared for bed. She watched him in the mirror as she brushed her long golden hair, watched him and realised this was the longest period since their first night of marriage that Luke hadn't made love to her. And already she felt desolate.

Her desolation increased as Luke turned over on his side once they were in the huge double bed together, his back turned firmly against her, the room in darkness. 'Luke?' she queried when she could stand the silence no longer. 'Luke, are you asleep?'

'Not yet,' came his muffled reply

'Are you going to sleep?'

He sighed. 'That is usually the idea when one goes to bed.'

'But I—Don't you want me?' She could make out his

bare back in the darkness, longing for the closeness of him, the male dominance of him.

'I thought you were tired?'

She sniffed miserably. 'I am, I suppose.'

Still he didn't move. 'You do not sound very sure.'

'I'm not, I—Why are you doing this?' She sat up in the bed, switching on her sidelamp. 'Because of that stupid argument we had this afternoon?' she demanded. 'But you must know I didn't mean it that way.'

He turned to face her. 'And this?' he indicated the chiffon nightgown she wore. 'Was this not meant as a deterrent?'

She gave a nervous laugh. 'Don't be silly!'

'You have not worn such a garment since our wedding night.'

'I know. But it just seemed—You haven't been very approachable tonight.'

'So you chose to wear that.' His disgust was obvious.

'Are you still angry with me?' There was a note of pleading in her voice.

'I was not angry, merely respecting your wishes. Oh, go to sleep, Sophie.' He turned on his side again. 'I would welcome a good night's sleep even if you would not.'

That put her firmly in her place. She turned slowly and switched off the light. She had made the first move and Luke had made it obvious he didn't want her. She wouldn't try again.

Sleep was a long time coming to her, her misery unshakeable. Luke fell asleep quickly, by the slow even tone of his breathing, making her resentment grow. She didn't think she could stand this marriage if Luke's physical warmth was to be denied her as well as everything else; it was the only thing that made this situation bearable.

She awoke to feel hands running caressingly over her body, hands she recognised only too well. She turned into

Luke's arms, raising her face automatically for his kiss. 'Mm,' she snuggled into him. 'I thought you didn't want me tonight.'

'I was wrong,' he growled. 'Perhaps in a few weeks' time I will be able to sleep meekly at your side, but not yet—*not yet*!' he growled, disposing of her nightgown by ripping it from her body. 'And there will be no more of those,' he said at her gasp of dismay. '*I* will keep you warm or you will remain cold.'

'Yes, Luke,' she smiled up at him dreamily.

'Do not be meek with me, Sophie, not tonight,' he said harshly. 'That is not what I want from you.'

There was nothing meek about their lovemaking that night; they hurt and loved each other until they fell into a deep exhausted sleep.

Sophie woke to find herself alone in the huge bed, only the tingling of her body and the discarded nightdress left to show her it hadn't all been a dream. She could hear no sound in the apartment but her own breathing, and a hurried search of the lounge and kitchen showed her that Luke had gone out.

There was no note, nothing, and all the joy went out of her. She didn't mean anything to Luke; her body did, but she as a person didn't. All that was left to her was to get on with trying to live the rest of her life, the life she would lead with Luke, his bedmate and later on the mother of his children.

The refrigerator needed stocking up if she were to take on the cooking of their meals, the apartment needed cleaning and a few homely touches added. She dressed in denims and a tee-shirt, sure that Luke would have returned by the time she got back with the food.

She quite enjoyed her shopping spree, her first real task as a housewife, although she had to get a taxi back to the apartment, as the four carrier bags of food were too much for her to carry alone. Luke would be wanting his lunch and she was so looking forward to cooking him the steak she had bought in a moment of extravagance. It wasn't exactly proof of her culinary expertise, but at least it should prove edible. After all, she had never told him she could cook!

She had difficulty undoing the kitchen door, her face flushed from her exertions. She could hear the murmur of voices from the lounge and wondered who their visitor was. Perhaps Luke would like her to take some coffee in.

She opened the kitchen door to find Luke's dark head bent over a golden female one, their murmured conversation making it impossible for them to hear her entrance. She didn't need to be told who the female was—Rosemary! She hadn't even waited a week before coming back into his life.

She turned to leave, but their conversation held her immovable. 'It was very clever of you, Luke,' Rosemary purred. 'I don't know how you knew.'

'It was not clever, Rosemary,' he replied softly. 'And I am glad that one member of this family knows why I married Sophie.'

'But how long will your marriage last under such circumstances?'

'I have no idea. Until she realises the reason, I should think. I do not think she will appreciate my motives.'

But she already knew his motives, and hated it. And fool that she was, she was still with him, couldn't leave him if she tried.

'She's a silly little fool,' Rosemary exclaimed, suddenly angry.

'Not a fool, just very young. She does not even begin to realise how I feel about anything.'

He was wrong, so very wrong. She knew exactly how he felt about her stepmother. God, she was torturing herself listening to this! She had to get out of here.

'Well, I'm glad you married her. I didn't think I would be, but now everything is working out perfectly.'

'I am glad. And I do not find my lot too hard to bear,' Luke said dryly.

Rosemary laughed. 'I'm sure you don't!'

Sophie had heard enough, and closed the door quietly to lean back against it for support. Oh God, back from her honeymoon one day and already Luke was seeing Rosemary! They had probably been out together this morning.

She collected up the shopping and left the apartment before her presence was discovered. They must never know she had overheard them, that would be too humiliating.

She escaped to the peace of one of the parks, watching the mothers walking their babies in their prams, the ducks paddling unconcernedly in the lake. Everyone seemed so happy in the midst of her misery. But what could she do? She had known of the affair before her marriage, had known of it and hoped that now she was Luke's wife it would stop. But did it really make any difference, did it stop her loving him and wanting to be with him? If she were truthful the answer was no.

She fed the ducks, unconscious of the amount of bread she had given them until she realised half the loaf had disappeared down their eager beaks. It must be getting late, she would have to return soon.

This time she made a great deal of noise about walking into the apartment, not wanting to interrupt anything more intimate than their private conversation. She was unpacking the shopping when Luke came into the kitchen, looking up briefly to give him a strained smile.

'Where have you been?' he demanded without preliminary.

She gave the shopping a wry glance. 'Isn't it obvious?'

'You have been gone hours,' he accused.

'A couple, maybe,' she acknowledged. She shrugged. 'We needed food, so I went shopping.'

'Why did you not tell me? I could have helped you.'

'You weren't around to tell,' she said abruptly, more sharply than she had intended.

'I was in my studio.'

Her hand hesitated on the refrigerator door. 'You were?' That was the one place she hadn't thought to look, not expecting him to be working.

'Of course. You did not think I had gone out and left you alone?'

'Well, I——'

He sighed. 'You did think that. I heard you moving about in the bedroom and then you had gone.' He picked up the half a loaf that remained. 'Have you already eaten?'

She gave a guilty laugh. 'I fed the ducks.'

He raised dark eyebrows. 'I am glad someone has eaten.'

'Are you hungry?'

'I seem to remember being asked that question once before by you. My answer is the same.'

She backed away from the look in his eyes. 'Not now, Luke,' she said breathlessly. 'I really am hungry. It's hours since we last ate. You must be hungry too. I didn't realise it was so late, almost one-thirty. We really should——'

'Stop making excuses, Sophie, I get the message!' and he slammed out of the room.

Oh God, she had done it again. She had been right to feel apprehensive about their return yesterday; the honeymoon period was indeed over.

Lunch was a strained affair, as were most of the meals they shared together over the next few days. The nights were even worse. Luke had meant it when he said she would remain cold if he didn't warm her—and he certainly didn't do that. He didn't touch her.

She telephoned her father on Thursday morning, inviting him to have lunch with her up in town. He agreed readily, much to her relief. Luke was out for the day, visiting a client, he had said, so she would have the pleasure of seeing her father alone. It would be just the two of them again.

Her father was already seated at their table when she arrived, his face lighting up with pleasure. 'Hello, poppet,' as he saw her seated opposite him.

His dear familiar face made her want to cry, although that really wouldn't do. She hadn't invited him here to burden him with her problems, she had just wanted to be with someone who loved her. 'You're looking well, Daddy.'

'Thank you, although the same can't be said for you. You look drained.'

She grinned at his honesty. 'Thank you, Daddy!'

'Well, you do. I know, I know, I shouldn't have actually said it. Married life isn't easy, is it?'

Not her married life anyway. She looked at him anxiously. 'Everything is all right between you and Rosemary?'

'Couldn't be better. Of course, she wasn't very happy about being left behind today,' he patted her hand, 'but I wanted to see my little girl alone, satisfy myself that you're really happy with Luke.'

Sophie frowned. 'Mummy is at home?'

He nodded. 'It's been nice having her with me for a change.'

'But I—I thought she was back in London.'

Her father accepted his glass of whisky from the waiter, watching her as she sipped her Martini and lemonade. 'She came up to town a couple of days ago to do some shopping, but that's all. Shall we order?' he indicated the menu.

Sophie made her choice in a dream. So Luke wasn't

seeing Rosemary today. Another woman, perhaps? Or could he really have been telling the truth when he said he was visiting a client?

She felt sure the meal was excellent, her steak in the mushroom sauce one of the tenderest she had ever had, but it might all have been rubber for all the ease with which she ate it.

'Is that not agreeing with you?' Her father was watching her as she pushed the food about her plate.

She came back to an awareness of her surroundings with a start. 'Agreeing with me?' she asked vaguely.

'Well, yes. I—I didn't know if perhaps—I remember your mother used to find certain things—not to her liking.'

Understanding dawned. 'Will you be very disappointed not to be a grandfather?' she asked gently.

'I'm not going to be?'

She shook her head. 'Not yet.'

He put down his knife and fork, taking her hand in his. 'You have plenty of time, Sophie. Is this the reason for your depression, the reason you sounded so desperate when you called me yesterday?'

Had she really sounded desperate? Perhaps she had, but that was the way she was feeling at the moment. But her father had enough problems of his own, he didn't need to be burdened with hers.

'I didn't mean to sound like that,' her smile was strained. 'I hope I didn't force you into coming up to town today.'

'No one could force me into coming to see my little girl,' he told her sternly. 'You know I've always been willing to listen to your troubles, helped you when I could.'

No one could help her in her mindless love for Luke, not even her father, she realised that now. 'I don't have any troubles,' she lied. 'Goodness, I haven't even been married two weeks yet!'

'Time is irrelevant. Something is bothering you. Luke is disappointed, is that it? I know these Latin types often put an emphasis on the wife producing a family as soon as possible. Is that what's wrong?'

'Nothing is wrong, Daddy, believe me. I was just missing you.' She squeezed his hand. 'And Luke isn't typical of the Latin type.'

'I suppose not. But I'm not happy about the way you look, Sophie. You aren't keeping anything from me?'

'Of course I'm not. Now let's choose a sweet.' She ate her peach meringue with a look of pleasure to please her father, although the sickly confection made her feel nauseous.

'Why didn't Luke join us today?' her father asked as they lingered over their coffee.

Because she hadn't even thought to ask him to! He never asked what she was doing, where she was going, and she had seen no reason to inform him of her movements today. 'He—er—he had to see someone on business,' she prevaricated.

'The honeymoon's over already, hmm?' he teased.

He didn't know how right he was! She shrugged. 'Luke has to work.'

'He's rich enough not to.'

'He enjoys his work.'

'Mm, well, I hope he isn't neglecting you.'

'Of course not, Daddy. This is the first time he's been anywhere without me since we married.' Which was true; he just spent all his time in his studio, only emerging for meals. 'He could hardly take me to a business meeting, now could he?'

'I suppose not,' he admitted grudgingly. 'But I'd like to have a word with him about the way you look.'

'You're giving me a complex, Daddy!' she teased.

'Damn it, he isn't taking care of you!'

'I'm big enough to take care of myself,' she soothed. 'Look, why don't you come back with me now and you can stay to dinner?'

'I have to look in on the office this afternoon, make sure they aren't robbing me blind,' he teased. 'And then I—I promised Rosemary that I wouldn't be late home, certainly in time for dinner.'

She bit her lip. 'I—I see. Oh well, another time.'

'Now don't look like that, Sophie,' he urged.

'Like what?'

'Like I just hit you.'

She blinked back her tears. 'Don't take any notice of me, Daddy. I'm a little emotional at the moment.'

'Only natural in your disappointment.' Anger entered his blue eyes. 'That husband of yours should be taking you out, not going to business appointments.'

'I really don't want a child yet, Daddy.'

'That isn't the point. I've a good mind to call Rosemary and tell her I'll be late back and come home with you. It seems to me that Luke needs a little plain speaking.'

'No!' Her voice was sharper than she intended. 'You promised Mummy, remember.' And any interference from her father would only alienate Luke even more.

'She would understand in the circumstances.'

'No, really, Daddy,' she gave a watery smile. 'Luke wouldn't like it.'

'I don't give a damn——'

'Please, Daddy,' she pleaded. 'Luke and I will work it out.'

'So you do admit there's something wrong?' he pounced.

She smiled. 'You should have been a lawyer instead of a businessman! I don't think you need to look in on the office, no one would dare to rob you,' she teased, 'you're too astute. But as you said, marriage isn't easy.'

'So you don't want me to speak to that stubborn husband of yours?'

'He wouldn't like it,' she repeated.

'Then come down for the weekend,' he encouraged. 'That way I could talk to him without making an issue of it.'

She was tempted, but the coolness between herself and Luke would be all the more noticeable in the company of other people. She wasn't ready to admit defeat to Rosemary just yet.

'Perhaps later on, Daddy,' she smiled. 'I'm not ready to share Luke yet.'

He drove her back to the apartment. 'You will call me if you need me?'

She hugged him, dreading going up to the apartment, to the coolness she would meet there. 'Don't worry, I always know who to turn to when I'm in trouble.'

He patted her cheek. 'Don't forget it.'

The apartment was in silence when she let herself in, although the used crockery in the kitchen pointed to Luke having returned at some time even if he wasn't here now. Sophie discarded her jacket and brushed her hair before going in search of him. After her mistake of last time she looked in the studio first.

'Luke——' She stopped in her tracks as she saw him bending over the female lying on the studio couch. His hand slowly left the woman's shoulder, the material of the gypsy-style blouse she wore pulled seductively off the smooth creamy flesh of that shoulder. Sophie hurriedly left the room as Luke turned to look at her, feeling sick with reaction. It *had* been another woman.

She hadn't gone far before she felt herself spun around, Luke's face livid with anger. There was something wrong here; *she* should be the one who was angry.

'What do you think you are doing?' he demanded, his eyes hard and cruel, a mocking twist to his sensuous lips.

Her eyes widened at his attack on her. 'What do I think *I'm* doing?' She was astounded.

His fingers bit cruelly into her flesh. 'That is what I said,' he nodded grimly.

'*I'm* not doing anything —except leaving!'

'Leaving?' he repeated sharply. His gaze ran slowly up and down her body in insolent appraisal. 'And where would you go?' he taunted.

The look in his eyes made her feel degraded and ashamed, as if he knew the effect his hands on her shoulders were causing. 'Anywhere away from here,' she flashed angrily. 'Anywhere away from you and that—that woman!'

'Madeleine?' he raised dark eyebrows.

'If that's her name, yes! I saw you touching her, caressing her—and right here in my own home too!' Her voice broke at the humiliation he put her through.

His eyes narrowed, his hands dropped away from her shoulders. 'I see,' he said slowly. 'And why should my touching Madeleine affect you?'

She gasped at his insensitivity. 'Because I'm your *wife*!'

'Are you?'

'Yes, I am. Just because you've chosen not to—not to exercise your rights——'

'My rights!' he exploded, more angry than she had ever seen him. He made a grab for her, pulling her up against him, her feet barely touching the ground, his face only inches away from her own as he glowered down at her. 'You consider that when I take you I take you as my *right*? And you get no pleasure from it, I suppose? You do not lie in my arms and beg for my body on yours?' His mouth turned back in a sneer. 'Would you like me to show you how you react to my possession? Would you?' He shook her hard.

'No! No . . .'

He thrust her away from him. 'Perhaps that is as well, I have no intention of *exercising my rights*. I do not want you!'

That, more than anything, cut into her, wounding her more than she would ever let him know. 'Luke, I——' She broke off, her eyes riveted on the woman standing in the open doorway of the studio.

The woman she knew only as Madeleine walked slowly into the lounge, a deliberate provocation to the swing of her hips. 'I hope I'm not interrupting anything,' her voice was husky and soft, her pouting lips an open invitation. She looked at Sophie with malicious enjoyment. 'Shall I leave?' she asked Luke softly.

'No,' he said tersely. 'At least, not alone. I will drive you home.'

Again those spiteful green eyes rested on Sophie. 'I wouldn't want to take you away from your wife.'

'You are not taking me away from anything.' Nothing of importance, his words seemed to say. He collected a bur-gundy-coloured leather jacket from the bedroom, shrugging it on over the black fitted shirt he wore with matching trousers. 'Nothing at all,' he added grimly.

He was almost at the door before Sophie found the courage to stop him. 'I—er—will you be back for dinner?' she asked breathlessly.

His hand rested at the redhead's elbow, his look impatient as he turned to look at Sophie. 'You said you were—going out,' he reminded her.

And he had ridiculed her, as he was ridiculing her now. 'I—I could have changed my mind.'

'Do not do so on my account.' He opened the door for Madeleine to pass through. 'I have no idea when I will be back, so if you do decide to stay in don't wait up for me,' he taunted.

The silence was deafening once she was alone. Luke had

been deliberately cruel to her, had in fact humiliated her—and yet she still loved him! That was the worst humiliation of all, her love for him. He had taunted her desire for him, flaunted another woman in her face, and yet still she remained here.

He didn't return for dinner, and she had no appetite herself, switching on the rarely used television set so that at least she wasn't sitting in silence. She delayed going to bed for as long as possible, knowing she would never sleep if Luke wasn't back, if indeed he came back.

By one o'clock she was convinced he intended staying the night with the beautiful Madeleine. She crept unhappily into the double bed they still shared, even though Luke never intentionally touched her. She curled up into a tight miserable ball, wishing the hours away until morning.

It must have been an hour or so later that she heard muffled sounds coming from the lounge. Luke! It had to be Luke. She was up and out of the bed before she had any time for thought, the transparency of her turquoise nightgown clinging to her body.

Luke was standing by the drinks cabinet, a glass of whisky in his hand as he slowly turned to look at her. 'Well, well,' he drawled, his eyes narrowed, 'my little wife come to greet me. And dressed so temptingly too!'

He was still angry, and by the smell of the alcohol eminating from him the glass of whisky was far from being his first. He smelt of stale cigarette smoke too, and she knew he didn't smoke. No, but the lovely Madeleine did!

'You're drunk!' she accused.

'Far from it, my dear,' he mocked, his smile unpleasant. 'And far from incapable too.' He took a threatening step towards her.

Sophie backed away, frightened by the determination she could see in his face. 'Where—where have you been?'

His smile deepened. 'Where do you think?'

Her mouth turned back. 'With Madeleine.'

He gave an inclination of his dark head. 'How right you are!'

'You—you've been with her?'

'Have I not just said as much?' He took a large gulp of his whisky, no emotion on his face as the fiery liquid burnt a path to his stomach. 'Why all these questions? I warned you what to expect before we were married if I did not find fulfilment in my own bed—with my own wife.'

'You mean you——' She gulped, unable to finish.

'What else did you expect, Sophie?' he demanded harshly.

'I didn't think you would really—I didn't think——'

'Well, now you know,' he snapped.

Yes, now she knew.

CHAPTER EIGHT

AFTER the things Luke had just said to her Sophie thought it only natural to assume he would sleep in one of the other bedrooms. She was wrong. After he had undressed and showered he came into their bedroom as usual, shedding the towelling robe to reveal his nakedness without embarrassment.

Sophie turned away from the beauty of his body, her cheeks burning as the image stayed in her mind. No man had the right to be so damned attractive, so physically magnificent, his body firm and taut, not an ounce of superfluous flesh anywhere on his muscular frame.

She moved to the very edge of her side of the bed as he got in beside her, the male warmth of his body reaching out to her against her will, his male scent inflaming her senses. The room was in darkness, her breathing necessarily smooth and even as she sought to convince him she was asleep. In reality her tears were drenching the pillow beneath her, she was unable to stop them as she fought for control.

'You are not asleep.' Luke's voice came to her out of the darkness, a statement, not a question.

She took a deep breath. 'No.'

'You are not tired?'

'I–No, no, I don't think so.' She hurriedly wiped away the tears staining her cheeks.

She was turned gently into his arms, her head cradled on his shoulder. His long fingers caressed her face, tilting her chin up so that she looked at him. 'Your face is damp,' he said softly, gently.

'I—is it?' Her lashes fluttered down on to her pale cheeks, the room in semi-darkness, Luke's eyes all too seeing.

'I have made you cry,' he said with a sigh.

There was no point in denying what was obvious, so she remained silent, curved against the hardness of his body, the first time he had held her like this in days.

'You made me angry,' he explained. 'For days you have made me angry. And today you offered the final insult,' he added harshly.

Sophie looked astounded. '*I* did? But I've hardly seen you all day!'

'That is true, and there has been little politeness between us of late. Tell me,' his eyes probed, 'what did you think this afternoon when you saw me with Madeleine?'

He thwarted all her efforts to break out of his arms, so she remained in his embrace like a trapped bird. She licked her dry lips. 'What did I think?' she delayed.

'Yes.'

'I thought—well, I thought——'

'You thought I had been making love to her,' his words cut through the gloom. 'Why did you think that?'

She trembled against him, remembering the way he had been touching the other woman. She felt his arms tighten about her. 'You were caressing her, touching her,' she said with remembered horror.

'I was touching her,' he admitted. 'Touching does not prove anything.'

'But you—you must have been kissing her,' she said desperately.

'I was not,' he denied grimly. 'Did you see any evidence of my having kissed her? Was there any lipstick on my face, on my lips?'

'Well . . .'

'I will tell you, there was not. Lipstick the vivid shade that Madeleine always wears cannot be hidden. I had not been kissing or caressing her,' he denied harshly. 'But I had been touching her. I was getting her to pose for me.'

'P—pose for you?' Her eyes were wide. 'You were painting her?'

'But of course. A studio couch is not my idea of the ideal place for lovemaking.'

'It was with me——' she broke off, her cheeks flaming with colour.

Luke's teeth gleamed whitely in the darkness. 'I seem to remember I carried you to my bed before it got that far.'

'But why didn't you explain that you were only painting her?'

'You said you were leaving me,' he accused.

'I didn't mean it.' There was a terrible lethargy invading

her body, every part of her aware of him as he lay beside her.

'Did you not?'

'Well . . . maybe at the time.'

'I was surprised to find you were still here when I arrived home just now.'

'Were you?' It was surprising how low and husky their voices had become, almost a whisper.

'I thought you had run home to your father,' he explained.

She was startled. 'To Daddy?'

'Exactly,' he said dryly. 'I thought you had run home to Daddy. I was surprised to find you had not.'

'I——' She didn't know what to say; she *had* run to her father in her trouble, but just to see him had been enough. 'You make me sound rather juvenile!'

'Not juvenile, just over-protected by your father,' he corrected. 'He cannot always be there when you are angry or upset, and I am pleased to see our marriage is not to be subjected to you constantly running to him for comfort.'

But she had, she had! 'I'm grown up now, Luke. I'm a married lady.'

'Yes, you are.' He pushed her back against the pillows, pinioning her to the bed with his body. 'You are married to me,' he said throatily.

She shivered with delight as he nibbled her earlobe, his tongue probing every sensitive contour. 'You said—you said just now that you'd been making love to Madeleine,' she reminded.

'Correction, I said I have *been* with her,' he murmured against her throat.

Her hands strayed across his muscled back of their own volition. 'It's the same thing,' she said weakly.

'Not at all. I have been to a party with Madeleine and

several of my other friends. I have been in their company, nothing more.'

'But you did say you would seek fulfilment elsewhere.' She retained a last hold on her sanity, his mouth exciting her until she wanted only him.

'Ah, now that I do admit to saying just now, but only as a means of self-defence. I came back to find you still here when I expected you to have flown, only to have you throwing accusations at me.'

'But you were out all evening. How was I to know what to think?'

'I was out all evening because I did not relish coming back to an empty apartment—as I did this morning. Where were you through lunch, anyway?'

'I—er—I went shopping and had lunch out,' she lied.

He wrenched her chin up. 'Is that the truth?'

'Why should I lie?' she asked with feigned indignation.

He shrugged. 'No reason, I suppose.' He gathered her close again. 'But I was glad to come home just now and find you here, although this,' he tugged at her nightgown, 'this I do not like.'

'Shall I take it off?' she offered eagerly.

'It is not necessary.' With a sharp tug he had ripped the garment from neck to hem. 'I have my own way of dealing with these things.'

Sophie giggled. 'I wish you wouldn't keep doing that.'

His lips teased and parted hers with sensuous passion. 'Do you?' he breathed against her mouth. 'Do you really?'

Her mouth opened to receive his kiss. 'No . . .'

'I thought not.'

'You're very arrogant,' she reprimanded softly.

'I have to be, I am your lover.'

'Luke . . .' she whispered.

'Mm?'

'Why have you stayed away from me for so long?'

'Because I was waiting for some sign from you that you wanted my lovemaking. I am afraid that tonight I have run out of patience.'

'I'm glad,' she sighed before his mouth took possession of her, his body soon following its example.

Sophie awoke the next morning with a feeling of well-being, a warm arm about her waist, Luke's body curved against her back. She smiled contentedly as she remembered their night together, and stretched her body with feline satisfaction.

Warm lips nuzzled against her throat. 'I thought you were never going to awaken,' Luke murmured softly.

'Did you have any special reason for wanting me to?' she teased lightly.

'Oh yes,' he said throatily.

She turned to face him. 'And what reason was that?' She caressed the dark hairs on his chest, running her tongue provocatively over her lips.

'I have plans for you,' he smiled down at her. 'Very important plans.'

'Mm?' She kissed his shoulder, her hands on his firm muscled back.

'Yes, very important plans.' He sat up, throwing the bedclothes off her naked body. 'I am waiting for you to go and cook my breakfast,' he grinned at the indignation on her face.

'Cook your . . . Why, you——!'

He leant over to slap her bottom. 'My appetite is not for you this morning. I did not have dinner yesterday and I am hungry.'

Sophie hadn't eaten dinner either, now she came to think about it, but it hadn't exactly been the first thing on her mind when she woke up. 'How mundane!' but she climbed out of bed.

'Not mundane at all.' Luke lay back, his arms behind his head, watching her as she put on a robe. 'How can I make love to you when I am almost fainting with hunger?'

'Worse than mundane, practical!' She pretended disapproval. 'And stop looking at me like that!'

He gave a slow smile. 'I am just wondering if I might perhaps have been a little hasty.' He made a lunge for her but she laughingly evaded him.

'Too late,' she taunted from the bedroom door. 'Breakfast in ten minutes!'

She moved about the kitchen, squeezing fresh orange juice and cooking bacon and eggs. She usually only had toast herself, but it was almost eleven and it was a long time since they had eaten.

She had the bacon nicely sizzling in the pan when the telephone began ringing. Before she could pick it up the ringing stopped and she could hear the sound of Luke's muffled voice through the closed bedroom door as he picked up the extension.

She went happily back to her cooking; the call was probably for Luke anyway. The table was nicely laid, the last piece of toast in the rack when Luke finally put in an appearance, dressed now in navy blue slacks and matching shirt.

Sophie's smile faltered and died at the look on his face. 'Is there anything wrong?'

He leant back against one of the units, his arms folded across his chest. 'Should there be?'

'I—Why , no. But you—you seem different.'

His brown eyes were narrowed. 'Different from what?'

'Just—just different.'

'Different from the fool who made love to you last night,

perhaps?' he snapped harshly.

'I—What do you mean?'

'Do not pretend innocence with me, Sophie. That was your father on the telephone just now.'

Her cheeks paled. 'Oh!'

'I notice you no longer feign surprise,' he sneered. 'He telephoned to ask if we would like to go down for the weekend—but then you already knew that, didn't you?'

'I——'

'And you did run to him yesterday. You lunched with him,' he accused.

'Yes, but——'

His mouth turned back. 'Do not make excuses, Sophie. Perhaps I should really give you a reason to run to him telling tales.'

She backed away from the violent anger in his eyes. 'I didn't! I only——'

'You only gave him reason to be so worried about you that he felt it necessary to see the two of us together, to judge for himself just how badly I am treating you. And to think that last night I told you how pleased I was that you had not gone to him with your troubles, that you were being adult about it. You even lied to me when I asked where you had lunched. You are not worthy of trust, so I will no longer continue to trust you. You will not go out alone any more, and you will tell me of any further contact you have with your father.'

'You can't run my life like that,' she retaliated. 'I'm not a child! I will not——'

His hand flicked out and struck her across the cheek. 'You will do exactly as you are told!'

Sophie held her reddened cheek, her surprise much greater than the pain, the slap given to put her down rather than hurt her. 'I won't! I——'

'Would you like me to hit you again? And with much more force this time.'

'You wouldn't dare!' Her eyes flashed angrily.

'Are you sure of that?'

She wasn't sure of anything, she hadn't believed he would hit her at all. Perhaps she had asked for it, but it didn't make the pain of humiliation hurt any the less. 'Aren't you afraid the marks of your brutality will show when we see my parents?' she taunted.

'Who says we are going to see your parents?'

She paled, her eyes deeply violet. 'You mean we aren't going?' Tears filled her eyes. 'You're going to keep me a prisoner here just because I didn't tell you I met my father yesterday? You can't do that, Luke!'

'I can, if I choose to. But I do not intend depriving you of your family, although your father can make what he wants of the marks on your face. I am not answerable to anyone for my actions regarding my wife.'

'Then we are going?' she asked hopefully.

'Yes,' he bit out shortly. 'We will arrive in time for dinner tomorrow.'

Things were so strained between them the next day as they drove to her parents' house that Sophie knew no one could be in any doubt as to the tension between them.

'Couldn't we at least try not to show my parents how disastrously our marriage is turning out?' she finally ventured.

Luke looked at her coldly. 'I do not intend living a lie to suit other people.'

'It wouldn't be living a lie,' her eyes pleaded with him. 'The antagonism is between us, I don't see why we should involve other people.'

'I do not intend involving other people, but I will not put on an act either.'

'All right, then don't,' she snapped, suddenly angry. 'Let everyone know   I don't care!'

'I am sure you do not,' Luke agreed tightly.

'There's just one thing I think you should know—my father thinks there's a certain coolness between us because I haven't managed to fall pregnant.'

He gave a harsh laugh. 'A child between us now would be a total disaster.'

'I know that,' she said fiercely. 'But Daddy mistakenly got the idea that was the reason we weren't getting on too well.'

'Did you tell him that was the reason?'

She shook her head. 'He just assumed it.'

'And why did you not tell him the truth?'

'Because I don't know the truth! All I knew was that you no longer wanted me.'

'That is not true, rather the other way round. You did not want my lovemaking. You made excuses.'

Because he had been with her stepmother that afternoon! 'There was a reason for that,' she said evasively.

'I would be interested to hear it. The other night proved you are not averse to me.'

'Did you doubt it?' she asked huskily.

Luke shrugged. 'I could not be sure.'

'I wasn't that. It was just that—I thought you might tire of me,' she lied.

'After only a few days of marriage?' he scoffed. 'Hardly likely.'

'Well, I didn't know that. I don't know much about men,' she added lamely.

'That is true,' he agreed immediately.

'Do you have to be insulting to me all the time?' she snapped.

Luke raised dark eyebrows. 'Insulting? I was not being insulting. Your knowledge of men *is* limited.'

'I'm sorry I've proved so unsatisfactory!' she flashed. 'I'm sure you would have preferred a wife versed in all the arts of love.'

'Not at all.' He wasn't drawn by her anger. 'I told you I wanted a virgin, someone to be a mother to my children.' He pulled her face round to look at her, his fingers gently touching her mouth. 'Your lip is swollen here,' he said thoughtfully.

'Yes!'

'I did this when I struck you?'

'Yes!' she answered even more vehemently, liking his touch in spite of herself.

His hand dropped away. 'I am sorry,' he said softly.

Sophie's eyes widened. 'You—you're *sorry*?'

'Yes,' his voice was stilted. 'I despise myself for resorting to physical violence.'

'Oh yes, of course,' she said bitterly. 'Why resort to physical violence when good old-fashioned lust would have silenced me just as effectively?'

'I do not understand.'

'Oh yes, you do,' she contradicted forcibly. 'You've always known the effect you have on me physically. Good grief, that was partly the reason you found it so easy to persuade me to marry you. I'm a complete fool where you're concerned,' she added disgustedly.

Luke's brown eyes swept over her coldly. 'Physical pleasure is not the whole of marriage.'

'Perhaps not, but it's all we've got.'

'Yes,' he agreed quietly. 'But matters are not helped by your lies.'

She gasped indignantly. 'I only lied because I didn't want you to be angry again. Telling you I'd seen my father would have done that.'

'Has it never occurred to you that your father may have marital difficulties of his own?'

Sophie gave a bitter laugh. 'He's always had marital difficulties.'

'But lately they have become more intense.'

'Oh, I know that—I also know the reason for it.'

'You do?' he probed.

'Of course I do, it's no big secret, is it?'

'It would appear not,' he said dryly.

'It's not something that can be hidden.'

'But if you know all this why have you given your father the impression that we are not happy together? That can do nothing to help the situation.'

'I don't intend *helping* the situation. Why should I?'

'Indeed,' he nodded abruptly. 'That is the sort of answer I would have expected a child to make. It appears that is what you are.'

'Don't start using my age as a weapon against me,' she snapped. 'I may be young, but you still wanted me.'

'Fool that I am,' he muttered in a strangulated voice. 'But I cannot begin to understand you.'

'Then that makes two of us—I don't understand you either.'

'You do not try to,' he told her curtly.

Her father greeted them with obvious warmth, Rosemary's greeting was much more welcoming than Sophie had expected. But then it probably wasn't meant for her; her being here meant Luke was here too. Nevertheless, she was taken aback by the warmth of Rosemary's kiss on her cheek, and completely puzzled by the happiness shining out of her china-blue eyes.

Rosemary straightened the curtains in the bedroom she had just shown them into, while Luke left the two women after depositing their suitcase at the foot of the double bed. 'You're looking pale,' Rosemary remarked abruptly.

'I—I'm a little tired—from the journey,' Sophie added hurriedly.

Her stepmother gave her a knowing smile. 'Honeymoons have that effect, don't they?'

'It was the journey,' Sophie repeated crossly.

Rosemary shrugged. 'If you say so. But if I were married to Luke I——'

'Well, you're not!' she interrupted sharply. 'He's my husband, not yours.'

Rosemary frowned. 'Your father said you were very tense, I didn't realise how much.' She sat down on the bed. 'Would you like to tell me about it?'

Sophie's look was scathing. 'You're the last person I would talk to about it!'

Her stepmother stood up, her movements jerky. 'I know we haven't always been the best of friends, and I know that it's mainly been my fault, but I had hoped things would be different now. If you could just understand that a lot of my bitchiness has been due to jealousy——'

'Oh, I know that,' Sophie cut in.

'You do?' Rosemary looked relieved. 'Then you know what your marriage to Luke means to me.'

'Yes!' She knew what it meant to her too—being second best.

'Your father would like it if we could try to be friends,' Rosemary added.

She felt sure Rosemary would like it too; it would allay suspicion. 'Yes,' she acknowledged unenthusiastically.

'I—I'm sorry about your baby, about your not having one, I mean.'

That made Sophie see red. 'Why does everyone assume that I wanted one?' she snapped angrily. 'I'm too young to have a baby. And I've only been married a couple of weeks.'

'In your case time doesn't seem to have been important. You didn't waste any capturing Luke.'

'Look, we both know that I followed you to Luke's

bedroom that night,' said Sophie coldly.

'It was the painting that condemned you,' Rosemary said softly.

'Yes,' she accepted dully. 'Now, if you don't mind I'd like to wash and change for dinner.'

Rosemary gave her a friendly smile. 'Of course. And if you do feel like a chat at any time you know where my room is.'

'Next to Daddy's.'

Her stepmother looked at her closely. 'A lot of married couples have separate bedrooms, Sophie, it doesn't mean they don't have a normal married life together. You and Luke may even decide to have separate rooms later on.'

They might as well now, for all the intimacy there was between them. Last night she had slept on her side of the bed, conscious of Luke's naked body beside her, his back turned towards her not encouraging any contact from her.

'Maybe,' she nodded agreement, doubting if there would be any 'later on' between Luke and herself.

'Has Luke finished your portrait yet?' Rosemary changed the subject.

'I have no idea.'

'Will he have finished it for your father's birthday, do you think?'

Sophie put the suitcase on the bed, snapping open its lid to begin unpacking the contents. 'You'll have to ask him. He's been working on another portrait this week.'

'Anyone interesting?'

She shrugged. 'Someone called Madeleine.' She sounded much more casual than she felt, her jealousy concerning the other woman was still very strong. But perhaps it wouldn't hurt Rosemary to know she had other competition besides herself.

'Madeleine Drury?' Rosemary queried sharply.

'I really couldn't say,' Sophie said uninterestedly.

'A redhead, with cat-like green eyes?'

'That sounds like her.'

Rosemary sighed. 'In that case, a little word of warning, Sophie. Madeleine has been after Luke for months.'

Sophie could have laughed out loud at the irony of her stepmother warning her about another woman being after Luke. 'I couldn't do much about it if he wanted her.'

'Don't be a fool,' Rosemary snapped. 'You may only have been married two weeks, but even that should have told you there are ways of keeping your man.'

'Is that how you've managed to hold on to my father all these years?'

Her stepmother was pale. 'Your father loves me.'

'And you love him,' Sophie sneered.

'Yes, I do. God, Sophie, marriage to Luke has certainly changed you!'

Sophie gave a tight smile. 'Hasn't it just!'

'I wouldn't let your father see just how hardened you've become. I don't want him worried or upset right now.'

'Why especially now?'

'You'll find out—later,' and Rosemary left, the smile still in her eyes.

It all sounded very mysterious to Sophie, and she wasn't sure she was going to like 'later'. Her father and Rosemary obviously had something they wanted to tell them. Oh God—she sank down on the bed—they couldn't be going to divorce after all these years, could they?

Just the idea of it filled her with dread. But no, it couldn't be that, her father wouldn't be looking so happy. She might doubt Rosemary's love for her father, but she could never doubt his for her.

No, there had to be some other explanation, something else that was causing that inner glow to her stepmother. She couldn't begin to guess what it was.

She was putting the finishing touches to her hair when Luke came into their bedroom half an hour later, looking at him expectantly for some sign that he approved of her choice of dress, the black silk jersey clinging to the rounded curves of her body, its seductive elegance given a more demure appearance by the high roll neckline. But Luke looked right through her after his initial glance in her direction and went into the adjoining bathroom to take his shower.

'Did you choose that colour deliberately?' he finally asked, buttoning the snowy white shirt across his brown chest.

Sophie was sitting on the bedroom chair waiting for him. 'What colour?'

'Black. Are you trying to ruin the evening before it begins?'

She frowned. 'Could my wearing black do that?'

He shrugged his shoulders into the iron-grey velvet dinner jacket. 'It could if it is a reflection of your mood.'

'Why should my mood matter to anyone?'

'Do not feel sorry for yourself,' he snapped. 'Self-pity is something I abhor.'

'Self-pity? But I——'

'You will do nothing to ruin your father's happiness tonight,' he ordered. 'I hope you did not upset Rosemary when she told you. I know how childish you can be.'

'Right now I don't know what you're talking about. What's Mummy supposed to have told me?'

Luke gave her a sharp look noting her genuine look of puzzlement. 'She did not tell you,' he stated.

Sophie shrugged. 'I don't know, do I? She may have done.'

'She did not,' he said with certainty. 'I should have realised. You are too calm—I must expect hysterics at least.'

'Then you tell me and let's get the hysterics over with.'

He shook his head. 'It is not for me to tell you.'

'You're making all this sound very mysterious, Luke.'

'There is nothing at all mysterious about it, as you will soon find out.'

'How is it that you know this great secret and I don't?' she persisted.

'Possibly because they are unsure of your reaction.'

'You aren't going to give anything away, are you?' she snapped impatiently. 'Oh, let's go down and get this over with.'

Luke grasped her arm. 'Do not make a scene in front of them.'

Sophie wrenched out of his grasp, glaring at him angrily. 'Don't treat me like a child! I can take whatever it is they're going to tell me.' If she could take his affair with Rosemary then she could take anything.

He sighed, straightening his cuff. 'I hope so.'

Only her father was in the lounge when they entered the room, pouring them both a drink. 'Rosemary should be down in a moment,' he told them, looking rather anxiously at Luke, she thought.

Really, all this mystery was making her nervous, and her father looked nervous enough for all of them.

Rosemary looked stunningly beautiful, the blue chiffon gown exactly matching the colour of her eyes, eyes that suddenly seemed to have lost that hardness to them. She went straight to her husband's side, raising her face for his kiss. After an embarrassed glance at Luke and Sophie he complied.

Sophie hadn't seen such open affection between them for

a very long time and she gave an involuntary start. Luke's hard fingers on her arm kept her standing at his side, her look of bewilderment met by one of cool assurance.

'Can I have a drink, darling?' Rosemary asked her husband.

Simon frowned. 'Are you sure you should?'

She pouted at him. 'Just a little one won't hurt me.'

'But the doctors said you were to take it easy.'

Doctors—what doctors? Sophie's bewilderment grew. Surely Rosemary wasn't ill? She hoped not. She and Rosemary might have argued in the past, but she was the only mother Sophie had ever known, and she didn't wish her harm.

'They also said I was to lead as normal a life as possible,' Rosemary continued.

'Yes, but——'

Rosemary squeezed his arm. 'If you really don't want me to then I won't,' she smiled at him gently.

'Well ... perhaps a little one,' he conceded. 'But you must take care of yourself.'

'Yes, darling,' his wife glowed up at him.

Sophie was thoroughly confused by now. Rosemary was obviously seeing a doctor for some reason, but her father's attitude didn't seem to point to her being ill, at least, not ill as she knew it.

'Are you unwell, Mummy?' She could contain her curiosity no longer.

'Not exactly.' Rosemary looked at her husband. 'Simon?' she prompted.

He gave a sheepish grin. 'I feel a little foolish at my age,' and he did indeed look very embarrassed. 'Rosemary isn't ill, Sophie,' he cleared his throat noisily. 'The truth of the matter is—well, she—we——'

'I'm going to have a baby!' Rosemary announced proudly.

CHAPTER NINE

To say Sophie was taken aback was an understatement. She was stunned.

'But I—I thought you couldn't have children.' She had known of the unhappiness Rosemary felt in the beginning of her marriage when year after year she didn't produce the child she had so desperately wanted.

'There was never any medical reason for it,' Rosemary explained gently.

Sophie licked her suddenly dry lips. 'I—I see.'

'Sophie is naturally a little overwhelmed by all this,' Luke put in calmly.

Her father gave him a grateful smile. 'Yes—yes, of course she is. I—I'm still a bit dazed myself. Rosemary only told me yesterday.'

So that was the reason her father had invited them down here for the weekend, even though she had asked him not to. He hadn't wanted to see Luke and herself together at all, but to tell them his news.

Rosemary was to have a baby! The idea shocked her, she had to admit it, but now she knew the reason for Luke's concern, the reason he had thought she would make a scene. Well, she wouldn't give him the satisfaction of being right.

She went forward and kissed her stepmother on the cheek. 'I'm very pleased for you,' she gave a strained smile. 'Very pleased.'

Rosemary looked at her uncertainly. 'Really?'

'Yes, really.' She turned to her father. 'You must be so excited!'

'Well . . . a little,' he admitted ruefully. 'Although I'm a bit old to be starting another family.'

Rosemary linked her arm through his. 'Of course you're not, you're in the prime of life.'

He grinned down at her. 'I thank you for that, but I know it isn't true.'

Their light chatter was giving Sophie time to gather her scattered wits together, time she badly needed. The shock was lessening now, the numb feeling beginning to fade. She couldn't fail to see how this baby was pleasing her parents, they looked the happiest they had for years, and she didn't feel quite so shut out because she had Luke. He had tried to warn her without actually coming straight out and telling her, and she could at least feel grateful to him for that, although his warning had come out as more of a threat.

Dinner wasn't as bad as she had imagined, her parents seeming to consider they had talked about the coming baby enough. Nevertheless, her excuse of having a headache at ten-thirty was a genuine one, probably due to the tension she had been under lately.

She was in bed pretending to be asleep when Luke came into their room fifteen minutes later, aware of him moving quietly about the room as he prepared for bed. The bed gave slightly as he climbed in beside her and she waited expectantly for him to turn his back towards her as was his usual practice lately.

'I know you are not asleep,' his voice sounded loud in the darkness. 'Your breathing is much too deep.'

'Quite the detective, aren't you?' she said tartly. 'Why have you come to bed now? You don't usually retire this early.'

'I could not stay downstairs while my wife came to bed, it would not be polite to do so.'

'It wouldn't have bothered me.'

'I am sure it would not,' he said dryly. 'But as I said, it would not have been polite.'

'I'm sorry if I've dragged you to bed,' she snapped.

'You never have to *drag* me to bed,' he murmured throatily, turning on his side to look down at her, his fingers trailing down her bare arm. 'I am usually only too eager to join you, and tonight is no exception.'

The intimacy in his voice was drugging, her headache long forgotten. 'You want to make love to me?' she asked breathlessly.

'As always,' he said throatily.

'Always, Luke?'

His lips caressed her throat. 'Do you doubt it?'

She nodded. 'Quite often.'

'I cannot make love to you when you make me angry. I could be quite brutal with you if I did that, so I find it wiser to leave you alone at such times. Unfortunately you often make me angry.'

'I don't mean to,' she whispered.

'That is part of the trouble, you have no idea when what you do makes me angry.'

Her hands moved out tentatively to touch him, feeling the shudder run through his body. Sophie smoothed his muscular back, her firm uptilted breasts against the roughness of his chest. 'Is this making you angry?' she breathed against his skin.

'What do you think?'

'I would say a definite no,' she teased.

'You would be right.'

Once again Sophie felt the magnetism of him carrying her along on a tide of passion, felt herself become weak and pliable as only he could make her. And yet she felt a certain amount of resentment towards him too, resentment that he should choose to use her whenever he wanted. Her wants and needs didn't come into it, and although he always gave her pleasure it was always when *he* wanted to make love, his manner towards her at other times barely civil.

As her resentment towards him grew so her desire died. She was being used, was merely a body to him, someone to provide pleasure for him whenever he was in the mood.

She began to struggle against him, her thoughts ones of escape. 'No, Luke,' she cried, 'leave me alone!'

There was a curious stillness about his body as he lay partly across her. 'What did you say?' he asked dangerously soft.

'I said no,' she repeated, surprised at her own nerve. It was a sure fact he wasn't pleased at what she had said.

'No—what?'

'No, I don't want you to make love to me,' she said bravely.

Luke levered himself away from her with barely suppressed violence. 'You are refusing me, after making the advances?'

'Yes.' She was unable to look at him, at the glittering anger in his eyes.

'You did it on purpose?'

'Did what?'

'Aroused me and now deny me,' he accused grimly.

'Not on purpose, no. I——' her eyes pleaded with him for understanding. 'I don't like being used,' she said lamely.

'Used?' he ground the word out. 'Am I not also being used? You do not love me, and yet you respond to me.'

'I——'

'You use me too, Sophie,' he snapped harshly. 'And now

you think you can turn me off like a schoolboy. And if I choose to take you anyway?'

'I couldn't stop you,' she said huskily.

'But you do not want me?'

Oh yes, she wanted him, but she wanted him with love, not lust. 'No,' she lied.

'Very well.' He rolled away from her, getting out of bed and pulling on his clothes.

'What are you doing?' She sat up in bed, unaware of the provocative picture she made in her nakedness.

He gave her an impatient look. 'What does it look like?'

'You're going out? Now?'

'Of course now,' he snapped.

'But——'

'I cannot sleep with you in that bed after what you have done to me.' He pulled on his jacket.

'But—but where will you go?'

'Anywhere away from you. Do not worry, I will be back in the morning before your parents are awake. But tomorrow we have some serious talking to do.'

'We do?'

'You must know we do!'

'Please,' she bit her lip, 'don't go.'

He stopped with his hand on the door. 'You have changed your mind?'

'No! No, I haven't,' she said more calmly. 'I—I just don't want you to go.'

'I have to.' The door closed quietly behind him.

Sophie didn't sleep at all, her heart was too heavy. She hadn't expected him to leave her—maybe treat her to his chilling silence, but not actually leave her. Where could he have gone this time of night? More to the point, what would her parents think if they knew?

She doubted Luke would continue his affair with Rosemary now, but there would be other women, she knew that. He had married her because of her father, was even willing to stay married to her because he desired her, but there would always be other women, other affairs. Tonight she had rebuffed him, refused him the one thing he wanted from her; would he now finish their marriage? They had to talk, he said, and she felt sure it would be an ultimatum on his part.

Luke didn't love her, had never spoken any words of affection to her, so why should she suppose he would want to continue their marriage when it could hold nothing for him? But did she want it to continue like this herself? There was no need to answer that question; her refusal earlier was answer enough.

What a dismal failure this had all been! But hadn't it been destined to be from the start, with no love on Luke's side and the love she felt for him unwanted. Perhaps it was better this way. Better for whom? She would die without Luke, without even the small part of him he was prepared to give.

Contrary to what he had said, Luke was not back the next morning before it was time to go down to breakfast. Sophie waited as long as she could, but by nine-thirty decided that one of them should at least put in an appearance.

Her father, the only occupant of the dining-room, put his paper away as she came in. 'No Luke?' he smiled.

'He—he's a little tired this morning,' she excused, sitting down opposite him. She poured herself some coffee. 'He's been working hard.'

He nodded. 'Your mother said he was working on another portrait.'

How did she—— Oh yes, she had told Rosemary so herself. 'More coffee, Daddy?' she indicated his half empty cup.

'Thanks.' He pushed his cup forward. 'Aren't you having any breakfast this morning?'

'No, I—I'm not hungry.' And she wasn't, food was the last thing on her mind. She was so worried about where Luke could be that she couldn't even think of food.

'Do you still have your headache? You're looking awfully pale.'

'Headache?' She frowned, her headache of yesterday evening quite forgotten after what had happened later. 'Oh no, it's quite gone.'

'Has this baby upset you?' he asked gently.

'The baby——? No, of course not,' she hastened to reassure him. 'You must be overjoyed.'

'Naturally I'm pleased, but——'

She put her hand over his. 'You don't have to play it down for me, Daddy. I can see how excited you are. I'm not a child, Daddy, I don't need to be humoured. I don't know why everyone had the idea that I would make a scene——'

'Oh, not a scene, Sophie,' her father cut in.

'But you did—you all thought that, including Luke.'

'Only because—well, you've been an only child for so long, my own little girl.'

'And now I'm a grown woman.'

'Yes, I suppose you are.'

'And it's time everyone realised it.' She smiled. 'I shall quite like having a baby brother or sister.'

'Oh, Rosemary's convinced it will be a boy.'

'I hope she isn't disappointed.'

'With her determination?' he grinned. 'It wouldn't dare be anything else!'

'Where is Mummy this morning?' Sophie asked. 'There's nothing wrong, is there?'

'No, no. I just like her to have a rest in the mornings. It isn't going to be easy having a baby at her age and I want her to take things as easy as possible. All this travelling up to London will have to stop, and the late hours she used to keep. She's no longer young to be having her first pregnancy and I wouldn't want anything to go wrong at this stage. She's so pleased about, it's made a different woman out of her.'

Sophie had noticed that, the more gentle look in her stepmother's eyes, the love she showed her husband. 'I—er—I was wondering, as Rosemary will stay here resting, I was wondering if she would like me to stay on with her for a while, a little feminine company, so to speak.' She gave him a bright smile.

'But surely—— You've only been married two weeks!' He looked astounded.

'I know, but——'

'Won't Luke mind?' he cut in.

'Oh, I'm sure he won't. He's very busy at the moment, I hardly see him.'

'Yes, but——'

'Ask him yourself, Daddy. I'm sure he would much rather have me out of the way at the moment.'

He frowned. 'Well, it doesn't seem right to me. This problem you were having,' he said sharply. 'It hasn't resolved itself?'

Well, one of them had; Rosemary was definitely out of the picture. But there were still the other women, there always would be. 'I think we may be better for a small separation,' she admitted reluctantly.

'After only two weeks of marriage?'

'I don't mean a separation as such, just a little while away from each other. Rosemary's condition would give me good reason for making the suggestion.' It would also save her the humiliation of having Luke ask her to leave. God, she was a coward! 'That is, of course, if you think Mummy would want me here.'

'I'm sure she would,' he said instantly. 'But I don't understand the reasons for leaving Luke.'

'I'm not leaving him,' she said sharply. 'Just having a few days away from him.'

'Are you sure that's all it will be?' he asked shrewdly.

Tears filled her eyes. 'Don't you want me here?'

He put his hand over hers, squeezing gently. 'It isn't that, Sophie. I'm just concerned for you. Surely that's only natural?'

'Of course, Daddy. But I—I need time away from Luke. Something is wrong with our marriage and I can't straighten it out with him.' *Some*thing was wrong with her marriage? *Every*thing was wrong with it.

'Pretty overpowering sort of chap, isn't he?' her father said ruefully.

'That's an understatement! He completely swept me off my feet before I had time to think.'

'I gathered that.'

Sophie blushed as she remembered the way her wedding to Luke had come about. But she *had* done the right thing— look at the happiness her father and Rosemary were now sharing. There couldn't be a happy ending for everyone.

'Yes, well, you know the old saying . . .'

'Marry in haste and repent at leisure?' her father finished for her. 'But I thought you loved him.'

'I do!' That was the tragedy of it all!

'Then why—— Oh, never mind, I don't suppose it's any of my business anyway. But you're welcome to stay here for as long as you want to, although I would prefer that you talk it over with Luke first. Who knows, you may be able to talk this thing out now.'

'I'll go up and talk to him now,' Sophie agreed. She had to find out if he was back yet anyway.

'Drink your coffee first,' he ordered. 'I'm sure he won't appreciate being woken up to be told you're leaving him.'

'I'm not——'

'As good as, Sophie.'

'It isn't like that, Daddy,' she evaded his searching eyes as she stood up to leave. 'I'll pop in and see Rosemary too.'

'Okay,' he nodded.

Sophie hurried up to their bedroom, certain that Luke must be back by now. She wasn't disappointed, she could hear him moving about in the adjoining bathroom. She had to approach this thing properly, wouldn't give him the satisfaction of knowing how much he had hurt her.

She was sitting on the bed when he came out of the bathroom, his only clothing a blue towelling robe, his dark hair still damp from the shower he had just taken. Nevertheless, he looked as drained as she did, with a white ring of tension about the firmness of his mouth.

He gave her a brief glance before starting to dress. Sophie looked away from the lithe nakedness of his body, maybe her last chance of seeing him so intimately. She might have told her father that she wasn't leaving Luke, but she had a feeling this break would be final.

'I expected you back before this,' she said tentatively.

'No one has noticed my absence?'

Except her! She had missed him terribly. 'I told Daddy you were sleeping in.'

'You have already seen your father?' His voice was taut.

'I've been down for coffee.' She turned back to look at him just as he began buttoning the dark brown shirt he wore.

'Rosemary was not there?'

'Daddy's insisted that she rest.'

Luke nodded. 'Very wise.' He tucked the shirt into the low waistband of the brown trousers he wore.

'Where did you go?' she asked.

'To a hotel.'

Her eyes widened. 'That time of night, without any luggage?'

'They did not seem to find it odd,' he said distantly.

'You didn't have to go anywhere,' she told him breathlessly.

His dark gaze passed over her scathingly. 'After what you had done to me I could not stay here.'

'But I didn't do it on purpose, Luke. I just—I didn't want to be used again.'

'You keep saying that word,' he snapped.

'It seems to be applicable.'

'If you choose to think so.'

'I could use the word lust if you would prefer it.' His cool arrogance was making her angry when she wanted to remain calm.

'I think perhaps I do—at least it seems to point to the same feelings on both sides.'

'Maybe.'

'There is no maybe about it,' he scoffed. 'But now we have to talk.'

Sophie stood up with jerky movements. 'There's no need for talk, Luke. I—I've decided to stay on here for a few more days.'

'You have *what*?' His voice was dangerously soft.

'I've talked to Daddy and——'

'You have talked to your father about this?' He swung her round to face him, anger in every taut line of his body. 'You have spoken to your father about what happened between us last night?'

'No! No, of course I haven't. I meant that I've spoken to him about staying on here a few days. Mummy has to stay and rest and I thought I might keep her company.'

His mouth turned back in a sneer. 'I have never known you to seek your stepmother's company before.'

'Then perhaps it's time I did!' Her violet eyes flashed her anger.

'A little late in the day for that, is it not?'

'Perhaps, but it's what I've decided to do.'

'What *you* have decided?' he queried softly. 'And what about me as your husband, do I have no say in the matter?'

'Of course you do——'

'I am glad to hear it,' he said dryly. 'Then I do not want you to stay here. I want you back in London with me, where you belong.'

'I said you had a say in it, I didn't say you could tell me what to do.'

He gave a harsh laugh. 'Then I do not have a say; you have already decided. Does your father not think it strange? Or have you told him about the excessive demands I make upon you, the amount of times I have wanted your body?'

Sophie was scarlet by this time. 'Certainly not!'

'Why not?' he taunted. 'I am sure it is what he suspects anyway.'

'That isn't the reason I'm staying here,' she snapped. Far from it!

'Forgive me,' Luke mocked, 'I thought it was my lust you did not like.'

'I just don't like the way our marriage is. I want a few days to sort myself out.'

He gave her a searching look. 'A few days? Are you telling me you will be coming back to me—eventually?'

'Maybe. I—I don't know, do I?'

'But you expect me to stay here the rest of the day acting as if nothing is wrong and then meekly leave on my own tonight? What do you take me for, Sophie?' he scorned. 'A fool?'

'No——'

'Then you will understand if I leave now.'

She clutched at his arm. 'I don't want you to go yet. Besides, I—I haven't spoken to Rosemary yet, she may not want me to stay.'

'And if she does not you expect me to take you back to London with me?'

Put like that it did sound rather a cheek. 'I didn't mean it like that. Oh, please don't go yet, Luke. Stay for lunch at least.'

He looked down pointedly at her hand on his arm and she hurriedly removed it. 'I will have breakfast and then make my decision. I cannot think on an empty stomach.'

'I'll go and see Rosemary while you eat.'

His dark eyes mocked her. 'Avoiding being with me at all costs?'

Colour flooded her cheeks. 'Certainly not! I told Daddy I'd look in on her.'

'Then you must do as you told *Daddy* you would.'

'Luke!' she looked up at him reproachfully. 'Why are you making this hard for me?'

'You expect me to make it easy?'

She shook her head. 'I suppose not.'

'Very well,' he wrenched open the door, 'then do not ask such stupid questions. Go and see your stepmother, we will talk again later.'

'You won't change my mind,' she told him hurriedly.

'I do not intend trying,' he retorted coldly. 'I do not make those sort of moves. If you want to stay here then you can stay here. But do not expect me to welcome you back if you should change your mind at some later date.'

She felt as if he had offered her an ultimatum, go with him now or not at all. But she couldn't go back with him, she just couldn't. 'I won't change my mind,' she said with quiet determination.

He nodded distantly, his face a shuttered mask. 'I will see you later.'

Sophie found Rosemary still in bed, propped up by several pillows as she flicked through a magazine. She put this down as Sophie came in, her smile one of genuine welcome. It was years since Sophie had seen her stepmother without the sophisticated make-up she favoured, and she couldn't help thinking how much younger and more attractive she looked without it.

'Come and sit down,' Rosemary patted the bed beside her.

Sophie did so, feeling a little awkward now that it actually came to making the suggestion to her stepmother. After all, she had only just moved out.

'It's years since you did this,' Rosemary smiled at her.

That was true. Sophie had grown out of visiting her stepmother's bedroom at an early age, mainly because Rosemary hadn't invited it. Maybe the baby had mellowed her. 'I—I've just been talking to Daddy. He—I—I wondered how you would like it if I stayed on a few days and kept you company. Daddy has his work to do and he says you have to stay here and take things easy, and I——'

'Calm down, Sophie,' Rosemary advised gently. 'I would love you to stay and keep me company. I know we've had our differences in the past, but I hope that's all over now. What I don't understand is your desire to be away from Luke so soon after your marriage.'

'Well, he's busy, and——'

Rosemary shook her head. 'You might get your father to believe that, but I'm not taken in so easily. I noticed things were a little strained between you on Tuesday, and then when you called your father on Thursday that seemed to confirm that something was wrong. Of course my bitchiness on Tuesday evening couldn't have helped the situation. It's no excuse, I know, but I've been so tense, just waiting for the result of this pregnancy.'

'I don't know how you kept it to yourself,' said Sophie.

'It wasn't easy,' Rosemary said ruefully. 'But I've had so many disappointments in the past that I didn't want to say anything until I was really sure. I came up for tests on Wednesday and they telephoned me with the result on Friday.'

Wednesday was also the day she had visited Luke! But then neither she nor Luke knew that Sophie knew about that.

Her stepmother gave her a sharp look. 'Is it anything that I've done that makes you want to leave Luke? I've been a real bitch to you since I found out about the two of you, and I had no right to be like that. Does that have anything to do with it?'

'No,' Sophie answered truthfully.

'Are you sure? Your father did rather pressurise this marriage. Although there was that painting,' Rosemary added thoughtfully.

'Yes.' Sophie stood up jerkily.

'Is your separation to be permanent or just temporary?'

'Permanent, I think. But don't worry, I'll find somewhere of my own in a few days. I just want to get myself together first.'

Rosemary frowned. 'If you leave Luke you will stay here. This is your home. But are you sure you really do want to leave him?'

'Yes,' Sophie said tensely. 'It's the only thing to do in the circumstances. Our marrying at all was a mistake—desire is very different from love.'

'And desire is all there is?'

Sophie nodded. 'And you can't build a marriage on that. You're right when you say Daddy had a lot to do with us getting married, the truth would have hurt him terribly. I'll leave you now.' She realised she had said too much, not wanting to embarrass Rosemary over her affair with Luke now it was over.

Luke had disappeared when she came down the stairs and she rushed into her father's study, her face flushed. 'Has Luke already left?' she asked breathlessly. Surely he could have gone, not without saying goodbye to her? Surely even he couldn't be that cruel?

Her father looked up from the papers on his desk. 'Not as far as I know.' He sat back in his chair. 'He said something about going for a walk.'

'Oh!' She couldn't help but show her relief.

'We had a talk over breakfast, and he seems to be of the same opinion as you, that you would be better for staying here for a while.'

Luke had wasted no time in voicing his approval! 'I told you he wouldn't mind,' she said with forced lightness.

'I didn't say he wouldn't mind,' her father watched her closely. 'He just thought it would be better for you.'

Like hell he did! She lowered her lashes so that her father shouldn't see her involuntary anger. Why couldn't Luke just admit he would be glad to get rid of her? She had no doubt she had proved an enjoyable bed companion, his response to her had shown her that, but there would be plenty of other women only too happy to supply him with such entertainment.

'Rosemary quite liked the idea.' She made no comment on Luke's opinion.

Her father frowned. 'Just because you're married it doesn't mean Rosemary is any less your mother. I don't like you calling her Rosemary.'

She blushed. 'Slip of the tongue, Daddy.' Because 'Rosemary' was how Luke thought of her stepmother. 'I think I'll go and see if I can find Luke.'

'You do that,' he nodded his approval.

She met Luke on his way back to the house, his expression cool as he slowly appraised her. 'I have decided to leave now,' he told her distantly.

Her shoulders slumped. 'Couldn't you just——'

'No,' he snapped. 'I have explained to your father why I must go, as I am sure you have explained to Rosemary. I can see no reason for delay.'

Neither could she, except that she didn't want to say goodbye to him. 'Aren't you going to say goodbye to my parents?' she attempted to delay him.

'It is not necessary. I have already spoken to your father and your stepmother is not down yet.'

'Oh!' She couldn't think of anything else to say.

He looked at her for a long silent moment. 'Very well,' he said finally. 'I will go now. My things are already in the car.'

'I—I'll walk to the car with you.'

He nodded his dark head. 'If you wish.'

Oh, she wished, she wished now she were going with him. She put her hand on his arm. 'Luke . . .'

'Yes?' His tone wasn't forthcoming.

Her hand dropped away. 'Nothing,' she mumbled.

They walked out to the car together, Sophie very much aware that this could be a final goodbye. Luke swung into the driving seat, leaning out of the open window to look at her. Now that it had actually come to it she didn't know what to say.

'Do not feel so bad, Sophie,' Luke broke the silence. 'A two-week marriage will soon be forgotten.'

'By you,' she accused resentfully.

'By both of us.'

'But it isn't over. I'm only staying here——'

He gave a mocking smile. 'Do not lie to yourself as well as everyone else. You will not come back to the apartment, we both know that.'

'I——'

'At least admit it to me, Sophie,' he said harshly.

'But I—— What about my clothes?'

He shrugged his broad shoulders and switched on the ignition. 'You can collect them any time you like.'

'Thank you,' she said stiffly.

Again he smiled, his brown eyes pebble-hard. 'But I would advise you to telephone first.'

'But I have my key,' she reminded him.

'I did not suggest you telephone first because I thought you would be unable to get in,' he taunted.

How could she have been so stupid! Of course, he could have anyone there with him, and he certainly wouldn't welcome her interruption. 'I'll call first,' she mumbled.

'Do that.' He revved up the car engine. 'Goodbye, Sophie.'

'Goodbye.'

CHAPTER TEN

SOPHIE had never known time to drag by so slowly, the last five weeks had seemed like five years. A new rapport had grown between Rosemary and herself, a closeness that had never been there when she was a child. But it didn't matter how kind her parents were, she missed Luke abominably.

There had been no word from him, nothing to tell her he was still alive even. She longed to go and collect her remaining clothes just so that she could at least see him, but she dreaded telephoning him and perhaps finding he was 'busy'. She longed to see him, but didn't think she was yet up to the humiliation of finding him with another woman.

Besides, while her clothes remained at the apartment their separation wasn't final.

She stifled a yawn of boredom, her sigh deep-felt. She had just been swimming in their pool, the scantiness of her chocolate brown bikini showing how much weight she had lost the last few weeks, her figure thinning to almost gauntness. Luke certainly wouldn't desire her body the way she looked at the moment.

Thinking of Luke she sighed again. What was he doing, who was he seeing? She knew she had no right to wonder these things, but it didn't stop her thinking of him day and night. That was a lot of her trouble, she couldn't eat or sleep for thinking of him. Her bed seemed so empty without him beside her.

Martin came out on to the patio. 'Mr Sedgwick-Jones, Mrs Vittorio.'

Mrs Vittorio! Amazingly that was her, in spite of everything. 'Show him out here, please, Martin.' She sat up, pulling on her thin cotton robe. 'Hi,' she greeted Nicholas. 'Join me,' she indicated the lounger next to her own.

Instead he chose to pull over one of the chairs. 'I came over to invite you to dinner this evening.'

'Well, I——'

'Hey, come on, Sophie,' he chided. 'How long are you going to keep refusing my invitations? I must have asked you over to dinner half a dozen times, and each time you've refused.'

'I'm a married woman,' she pointed out.

'So?'

'So people would talk if I came over to your house.'

Nicholas sighed. 'My mother is an adequate chaperone—more than adequate,' he added dryly. 'And I would really like you to come.'

She felt sure he would; his pursuit of her did not seem

to have abated at all. To him her brief marriage might as well not have taken place. Perhaps that was the way she should look at it too, try to forget it ever happened. But how was she supposed to forget Luke, how *did* you forget the man you loved!

'I really don't think it would be a good idea, Nicholas,' she refused him.

'I don't see why not. Your marriage to Vittorio is over, isn't it?'

Like everyone else Nicholas had been told she was only staying a few days, but her parents had persuaded her to stay on instead of finding somewhere of her own, giving rise to much gossip, she felt sure. 'It isn't over, Nicholas,' she began carefully. 'We're just——'

'Separated,' he finished with satisfaction.

'In a way,' she admitted reluctantly.

'Then come over to dinner,' he grabbed hold of one of her hands, refusing to let go as she struggled against him.

She shook her head. 'It wouldn't be fair—to you. Just think of the gossip.'

'For once I don't care. I've always been mad about you, Sophie, you know that.'

'That's exactly the reason I don't think it would be a good idea.'

'I still want to marry you.'

'That could be a little difficult,' she said dryly, 'when I'm already married.'

'You could always divorce him.'

'Luke said there would be no divorce.'

'He won't have any say in it if we can find grounds for it.' His mouth turned back. 'And sooner or later he's going to give you grounds. It would just be a matter of proving it.'

Sophie was horrified. 'You're surely not suggesting I put someone on to watch him?'

Nicholas shrugged. 'Why not? If he won't let you go any other way . . .'

'I really don't think——'

'All right, we won't talk about it any more just now. But do come to dinner this evening. As a matter of fact I've already told my mother you'll be there.'

'You had no right to do that,' she said angrily, at last managing to snatch her hand away.

'My last method of persuasion,' he grinned. 'You wouldn't make me look a fool by having to tell her you aren't coming?'

Sophie smiled reluctantly. 'You never used to be so devious, Nicholas.'

'Then perhaps I should have been.' He stood up to leave. 'Then you might not have made the mistake of marrying Vittorio. It would have been better all round if you'd just had an affair with him.'

'Nicholas!'

'Well, it would.' Colour entered his cheeks. 'Not that I would have liked that either, but this way you could be tied up for years.'

'I'm not making any promises even then, Nicholas,' she warned gently.

He nodded. 'It's only natural that you should feel this way—once bitten twice shy, so to speak. But I would be a very different proposition from Vittorio.'

That was the trouble; he had none of Luke's fire and sensual attraction. But perhaps that wasn't such a bad thing. With Nicholas she would have a pleasant smooth-running marriage, with none of the feeling of living on a knife's edge that marriage to Luke had induced. It was like comparing water to champagne—and she had no doubt which one she preferrred.

'It wouldn't work, Nicholas,' she told him.

'Not now perhaps, but later, when you're over him. I can be very patient, Sophie, if I have to be. And I do want you for my wife.'

'I——'

'Don't refuse me now, Sophie. Wait a while, see how you feel then. We'll just be friends for now, nothing more.'

As far as she was concerned that was all they had ever been, although she had the feeling she had misjudged him somewhat. Maybe he had always seemed dull and boring to her because he was shy; he certainly wasn't acting boring and dull now.

'I'm not really sure . . .' she began.

'You wanted me to kiss you once, Sophie,' he reminded her. 'And I was stupid enough not to accept.'

She remembered the occasion vividly—and her humiliation. 'Luke explained about that,' she said huskily.

'Yes, he did, but at least it proves you aren't immune to me.'

All it seemed to prove to her was that she had attempted to hit out at Luke and failed. She could still remember the way he had laughed at her.

She sighed. 'It doesn't prove anything, Nicholas. I don't think——'

'I don't want you to think,' he cut in. 'I'll be calling for you this evening at seven-thirty.'

'But——'

'Seven-thirty, Sophie.'

Her own misgivings were strongly echoed by her father when she told him she would be dining out that evening. 'Is that wise?' he asked with a frown.

'Wise?' She pretended not to understand him.

'He may expect more from you now than you're prepared to give.'

She blushed scarlet. 'What do you mean?'

'I think you know, Sophie.'

'Oh, but Nicholas wouldn't—I wouldn't let him!' she said indignantly.

'I hate to say this, Sophie, but I feel I have to. You've been married, you've become used to a certain—well, a certain relationship.'

She coloured anew. 'I would hardly call two weeks long enough to get used to that!'

'But we all know it was longer than two weeks. You haven't forgotten the reason for the hasty marriage.'

Momentarily she had, at least her father's version of it. 'No,' she admitted quietly.

'Then you'll understand my fears. I wouldn't want you to rush into another relationship without giving it proper thought.'

'You're beginning to make me sound like a wanton woman, Daddy,' she teased.

'Not at all,' he denied hastily. 'I just want you to recognise the dangers involved in seeing Nicholas.'

'I do, Daddy.'

'And if you do ever go back to Luke? How do you propose to explain away seeing Nicholas?'

The same way he would explain his other women! 'I won't be going back to Luke,' she said firmly.

He gave her a sharp look. 'You've definitely made up your mind?'

'Yes.'

'Don't you think you should talk to him before you make such a big decision?'

She would like nothing better, but it would hurt too much. 'I don't think so, Daddy.' She looked at her wristwatch. 'I must get ready to go out.'

He put a restraining hand on her arm. 'Don't act too hastily, Sophie,' he pleaded. 'Give Luke a chance.'

'A chance to explain away his other women?' she snapped without thought. 'Oh yes, Daddy,' she added with a sigh, 'there've always been other women.'

'I see,' he bit his lip, shrugging. 'Well, I tried.'

'Yes, you did, and I'm grateful to you. Now I must get ready.'

Nicholas's mother obviously hadn't yet forgiven Sophie for marrying someone other than her son, although she began to mellow a little over their coffee in the lounge. Sophie almost heaved a sigh of relief as the conversation began to flow a little easier. Nicholas had smoothed over a lot of his mother's barbed comments, but it had been a little wearing on the nerves.

'Your mother is keeping well?' she asked.

'Very well,' Sophie confirmed.

'Of course I told Nicholas you weren't just staying at home to look after your mother. Now I've been proved right.'

'Yes,' Sophie acknowledged tightly, sure there was nothing this woman liked more than to be right.

'Nicholas tells me there could be some difficulty about a divorce.'

'Mother——'

'Don't interrupt, Nicholas,' his mother snapped. 'I suppose an annulment is out of the question?' she addressed Sophie.

After the honeymoon they had spent together! 'Definitely,' she confirmed, resenting this woman's intrusion into her personal life.

Mrs Sedgwick-Jones' nose wrinkled with distaste. 'I thought so. He didn't look the sort of man not to have taken full advantage of having a wife.'

'Look, I really don't——' began Sophie.

'*You'll* have to divorce *him*, of course,' she continued as if

Sophie hadn't spoken. 'I wouldn't want Nicholas to be named in a divorce.'

'Now look——'

'Mother——'

'It will all have to be carried out very quietly,' she carried on, ignoring their protests. 'It wouldn't do to start your married life under a cloud.'

'I really think you're——'

'Mother!' Nicholas cut off Sophie's protest this time. 'Don't interfere,' he ordered.

She looked as if he had struck her. 'Well! I was only trying to give you both a little sound advice.' She folded her arms across her immense bosom. 'But I realise that to you I must just seem like an interfering old woman.'

She had deliberately set out to make Nicholas feel uncomfortable, and she had succeeded. 'I didn't mean that, Mother, and you know it.'

'I'm sure I don't know any such thing. If a mother can't try and help her child then it's a poor world we live in.'

Sophie stood up to leave before the woman broke down and cried just for good measure. 'I think you have the wrong impression of Nicholas and myself,' she said stiffly. 'We aren't getting married, not now or in the future.'

'But——'

'And whether or not I divorce my husband is surely up to me and me alone,' she continued. 'Now, if you'll excuse me, I have to be going. Thank you for dinner.'

'Well, you ungrateful girl! I'm sure I was only trying to tell you what was best.'

'For whom?' Sophie demanded angrily. 'Certainly not for me. You can have no idea as to the state of my marriage, only my husband and I know that. I have no intention of divorcing Luke.'

'But Nicholas said——'

Her angry gaze swept over the two of them. 'Nicholas seems to have said altogether too much, Mrs Sedgwick-Jones. I like your son, I like him very much, but I am certainly not going to marry him.'

'Well!' and for once the woman seemed at a loss for words.

'Now I really do have to go,' Sophie said politely. 'Excuse me.'

Nicholas caught up with her in the driveway. 'Let me drive you home.'

She was grateful for the offer, having made her grand exit and realising she had no way of getting home except to walk there, but she didn't know if she should accept it. Nicholas seemed to have read far too much into her acceptance of his dinner invitation, and she didn't want him to think she was encouraging him if she accepted this offer of a lift.

'Come on, Sophie,' he encouraged. 'We can talk on the way.'

Perhaps that wouldn't be such a bad idea, at least she could finally try to convince him of her sincerity when she said she couldn't marry him. 'Very well,' she nodded coolly.

'I know Mother was a bit heavy-handed,' he began once they were on their way, 'but——'

'Heavy-handed!' Sophie scoffed. 'She couldn't have been any more blunt if she'd tried!'

He grimaced. 'Oh, but she could. She doesn't approve of my wanting to marry a divorced woman.'

'But that's the whole point, Nicholas,' she turned in her seat to look at him. 'You aren't going to marry me. You shouldn't have deceived your mother in that way. I consider you wholly to blame for tonight's embarrassment.'

'It was wishful thinking, Sophie.'

'And that's all it can ever be,' she said gently, her anger evaporating. 'I did try to explain to you this afternoon, but you wouldn't listen.'

'I guess I didn't want to. When he told me the two of you were getting married I felt as if the bottom had fallen out of my world. But when I found out you were living apart I—well, it gave me new hope. I suppose I just hoped too much.'

She bit her lip. 'I'm sorry. I never meant to hurt you.'

'But you're in love with him,' he said dejectedly.

'Yes.'

'Then why—— Sorry, I'm interfering again.'

'Why leave him?' Sophie finished with a slight smile. 'It's quite simple, Nicholas. He doesn't love me.'

'But he married you!'

'Not because he loved me. No, it was a much more basic emotion than that.'

'Oh!'

She could see she had embarrassed him again. 'Sorry, but you did ask.' She squeezed his arm. 'Thank you for bringing me home. And I hope I haven't made things too difficult for you with your mother.'

He shrugged. 'No more difficult than usual. She isn't an easy person to live with.'

No, she could imagine she wasn't. 'Thank you once again,' she said.

She made as little noise as possible going to her room, not that she thought she would disturb anyone, but because she wanted to be alone to think.

She had thought of Luke a lot the last five weeks, had thought of nothing else in fact, but she had tried to avoid analysing her feelings towards him. But talking to Nicholas and his mother she had discovered that she didn't want to be apart from Luke any longer, was prepared to take the little he had to give her. Who knew, her love for him might one day penetrate through his physical desire for her and he would perhaps feel a small measure of love for her.

But he had told her he wouldn't take her back, and he had meant it. He could even now have someone else living in the apartment with him. There was only one way to find out—go and see for herself.

It wasn't an easy decision to come to, to risk humiliation much worse than anything else she had ever known. But they had never had that talk Luke had suggested they have, never actually sat down and discussed anything. She thought it was time they did so.

She turned from removing her make-up as there was a gentle knock on her bedroom door, smiling at Rosemary as she came into the room.

'I thought I heard you come in.' Rosemary came to sit on the bed, watching her ministrations. 'You're back early.'

'I should never have gone.' Sophie smoothed her newly cleansed face. 'Nicholas's mother instantly started talking about my divorcing Luke and marrying Nicholas, and you know how I feel about that.'

'Divorcing Luke or marrying Nicholas?'

Sophie blushed. 'Marrying Nicholas.'

'Does that mean you're no longer sure about this separation from Luke? Your father said——'

'I've changed my mind since I spoke to him,' she cut in hurriedly.

'Since earlier this evening?'

'Yes.'

'Well, that's what I wanted to talk to you about, actually. Something you said to your father has been troubling me.'

'What's that?' asked Sophie.

'Well . . . You told him that Luke has other women.'

'Yes,' she agreed stiffly.

'Well . . .' again Rosemary hesitated. 'Do you really believe that?'

'I know it,' Sophie mumbled.

'Am I one of these women?'

Sophie was taken aback by the bluntness of the question. She cleared her throat noisily. 'I—It——'

Rosemary was very pale. 'Oh God, I am!' She shook her head. 'All this time you've been thinking that Luke and I . . . Oh God!' she said again. 'No wonder you couldn't bear to stay with him any longer! But it isn't true, Sophie, none of it's true.'

Sophie was just as pale by this time. 'What do you mean?'

'I mean that there's never been anything between Luke and myself that hasn't found its roots in my imagination. Luke would never involve himself with a married woman, and I would have probably run a mile if he'd made any moves in my direction.'

'But I—— What about all those times you said you were going to meet him?'

'It was never intimately. We always met as a crowd, at a party or half a dozen or so of us going to the theatre. I let you think I was meeting him alone because it made me feel young and attractive.'

'You aren't exactly old!' protested Sophie.

Rosemary sighed. 'I know that, I've just felt it at times. You see, I'd been a failure to your father——'

'I'm sure he's never thought so. He loves you, he's always loved you.'

'But I hadn't given him the son he so badly wanted. You can have no idea how inadequate that made me feel. I resented you because he doted on you. Things became a little easier when you went away to school, there was no constant reminder of my childless state.'

'I'm sure it never bothered Daddy that much.'

'Maybe not, but the seeds of resentment were there and I couldn't do anything to stop it. Then two years ago you left school completely, I couldn't take it and began to spend more and more time in London. There were plenty of men there who would have been only too willing to start an affair, but I chose to go after Luke.' Rosemary gave a wry smile. 'The reason I chose him was because I knew I would never get him. But I wasn't prepared for his reaction to you,' she added with a shake of her head.

Sophie licked her dry lips, shocked and upset by all that Rosemary was telling her but realising that in a way she was to blame. She had often shut her stepmother out of the closeness between her father and herself, had done it without realising it, never knowing how much Rosemary had been hurt by it. She felt sure her father was just as ignorant of the facts.

'His—his reaction to me?' she queried.

'Mm,' Rosemary smiled. 'He seemed to take one look at you and that was that. The elusive Luke Vittorio had fallen in love with you. It seemed the final straw, the two men in my life both seeming to prefer you to me.'

'Luke isn't in love with me,' Sophie told her quietly.

'Of course he is,' Rosemary scoffed. 'Oh, I know he's never told you so, but he's told me.'

'W-when?'

'The day I went up to London for my tests. I called round to see you both, but only Luke was at home. We had quite a chat. He knew from the first that my outrageous behaviour in chasing him was due to my jealousy of your closeness to your father.'

'But that night—that night I followed you to his room?'

'An act of desperation on my part. I knew he'd fallen for you and I didn't like it. I thought that if I—well, never mind what I thought, one look at that painting was enough to tell me what I wanted to know. I hated the fact that you were going to marry him, hated it, and bitchily told you he would always be mine.'

'And I believed you,' Sophie said dully, so many things explained now. But could it really be true that Luke loved her? It didn't seem possible.

'I can see that now,' Rosemary sighed. 'I forgot I'd ever said it. You see, Sophie, your marriage to Luke suddenly seemed to give me a happiness I hadn't felt since your father and I were first married. Suddenly we were alone and—well . . .' she blushed prettily. 'I suppose this coming baby shows you that things were right between us again. After all these years . . .'

'And Luke knew all this, that I was to blame for the strain between you and Daddy?'

Rosemary nodded. 'He's very astute.'

Sophie could see it all now, could see the misunderstandings there had been, the times they had talked at cross-purposes, she believing him to be talking about his affair with Rosemary and he believing her to be talking about the rift she had caused in her parents' marriage, however unwittingly.

'Oh, Mummy,' her voice broke, 'I have to go and see him, have to explain.'

'Explain what? That you love him? You do love him, don't you?'

'Yes,' she admitted huskily. 'Why did he never tell me how he felt, why let me think he only wanted——'

'Your body,' Rosemary finished dryly. 'Don't be embarrassed, Sophie. I told you we had quite a chat. He said that love was something you didn't want from him. But that isn't true, is it? These last few weeks you've been pining away for him.'

'I wanted his love so badly that I had to leave him,' she said ruefully. 'It was hurting me too much to love him and think he only felt desire in return.'

'Then go and see him and tell him so.'

'I intend to.'

Sophie didn't bother to telephone the apartment to tell Luke of her visit, wanting to see his reaction to her appearance without him having prior knowledge of her arrival. He could be very adept at hiding his true feelings, she knew that now.

She had risen very early this morning, and the train journey down here had seemed never-ending. She was pale and thin, but the purple dress she wore managed to conceal this somewhat. Her tenseness reached breaking point as she entered the apartment building, barely conscious of acknowledging the doorman's polite greeting.

The apartment was in silence, a completely unlived-in look about it. Dust covered the furniture, a quick look in the kitchen showing her the emptiness of the refrigerator. She slumped down in a chair. Luke wasn't here! It was something that hadn't occurred to her, even though she knew he often travelled abroad.

What could she do now? She had no idea how long he was to be away. She could always stay here; the apartment looked as if it could do with a good clean, and if she were living here when Luke returned he could hardly throw her out.

She heard a crash from the direction of the studio and jumped to her feet. Someone was here. It *had* to be Luke! The sight that met her eyes when she entered the studio stopped her in her tracks. Far from being away, Luke was lying on the studio couch, a dark growth of beard on his chin.

Standing on easels in front of the couch were the two

paintings of her, one of them the nude Rosemary and her father had been so shocked by, the other the portrait painted for her father. Luke had been right, it was the best work he had ever done—and had surely been painted through the eyes of a man in love? Oh God, she hoped so!

Sophie walked over to stand in front of the couch on shaking legs, feasting her eyes on him. His black hair was ruffled and untidy, but even so she could see it was much longer than he normally wore it, and he was very pale, deep lines etched beside his nose and mouth, a frown on his face even in sleep.

But what was he doing living amongst all this debris, the usual tidiness of the apartment completely erased? Well, whatever his reasons he couldn't continue to live like this. Sophie went into the bathroom, wetting the face-cloth and coming back to squeeze the surplus water over his face.

At first there was no reaction, then she saw his eyes flicker and open, his mouth turning back in a grimace. 'What the——' he blinked rapidly, focusing on her with effort. 'Oh no,' he groaned, 'not again! Just go away, Sophie. Leave me alone.'

It wasn't exactly the reaction she had been hoping for. 'I have no intention of going anywhere until I've cleaned this place up.'

'You mean . . .' he licked his dry lips. 'You mean you are real?'

'Of course I'm real. What's the matter with you, Luke? Are you drunk?' she asked suspiciously. 'Boy, it must have been some party! Have you just got home?'

He struggled to sit up, his clothes wrinkled and untidy. 'I have not been anywhere.' He shook his head dazedly. 'I have not been anywhere for days, weeks.'

'But you—there's no food in the apartment. You must have been out.'

He shook his head. 'No.'

'But what have you been eating if you haven't been out?'

'I have not been eating,' he grimaced. 'But I have been drinking. If you look under the couch you will probably find a lot of empty whisky bottles which I had sent up. There is more in the bedroom, but you will find no food.'

As she stepped back her foot did in fact catch on something and she heard the crash of glass against glass. Her mouth tightened. 'Get up, Luke,' she ordered. 'Go and shower and I'll get some food sent in. You look as if a good meal wouldn't come amiss.'

He ran a hand over his eyes as if they hurt him. 'I am not hungry,' he said tersely. 'Will you just get out of here and let me sleep.'

'Sleep is the last thing you need right now!'

'What do you know about it?' he snapped.

'I know you can't continue to live like this—you'll kill yourself!'

'Why are you here?' he demanded angrily. 'You were supposed to call first.'

'I wanted to surprise you.'

Sighing, he stood up, his clothes in an even worse state than she had thought. He didn't look as if he had changed them for days. 'Oh, you did that,' he admitted grimly.

Sophie was surprised to see how thin he was, his body almost gaunt. 'Oh, Luke!' She ran to him, putting her arms about his waist and holding him close against her. 'Luke, what are you doing to yourself!'

He wrenched her arms away from him. 'If you must stay here, Sophie, go and get that food. I want to shower and put on clean clothes.'

'But——'

'Leave me, Sophie.' His eyes were chilling. 'At least let me be clean so that I can face you on an equal footing.'

'Very well.'

She decided to go out herself and get a few provisions,

and found Luke sitting in the lounge when she returned, his face buried in his hands as he sat hunched over. He was dressed and shaved now, still much too thin, but more like the Luke she loved.

She put the shopping down and ran to kneel in front of him. 'Luke, what's wrong?'

He looked down at her with dazed eyes. 'You have come back. I thought you had gone.'

She clasped his hands in her own. 'Only to get some food, darling. I——'

'What did you call me?' he cut in harshly.

'Darling,' she repeated huskily.

He tilted her face up to look at him. 'Do you mean it?'

'I've always meant it.' Now wasn't the time for pride. 'Luke, why did you marry me?'

'You know why.'

'The real reason,' she prompted.

'I do not——'

'I've been talking to Rosemary,' she told him. 'She told me quite a lot of things, explained away a lot of misunderstandings.'

He stood up forcibly. 'And that is why you are here?'

Sophie still sat on the floor. 'No. I——'

'Because I do not want you here simply because you have listened to your stepmother.'

She stood up. 'I was coming here today anyway.'

His eyes narrowed. 'Why?'

'Because I—well, it's difficult to explain. Yesterday I went to dinner with Nicholas. His mother talked a lot about my divorcing you and marrying Nicholas.'

If anything Luke went even paler, his skin almost grey. 'So you are here to talk about a divorce.'

'No, I'm not! To have it actually put into words made me want to come and see you and find out exactly how you felt about me. Rosemary only spoke to me after I'd made up my mind to come here today. You see,' she twisted her hands together nervously, 'I believed you to have been having an affair with her all this time.'

'I know.'

Her violet eyes widened. 'You know?'

Luke nodded. 'At first I could not believe you could think such a thing, and then it just made me angry. I once told you that you had no idea what you did to make me angry—that was the main thing.'

'But why didn't you explain, tell me it was all her fantasy?'

He shrugged. 'I wanted you to ask me, to show you trusted me enough to believe me when I gave you the answer. But you never asked,' his voice hardened roughly, 'never gave any indication that it mattered enough to you to ask.'

'It mattered too much. I dreaded the answer. I—I love you, Luke.'

She could see the tension in his body. 'What did you say?' he grated.

Her eyes were swimming with tears. 'I love you. I love you!'

Luke took an involuntary step towards her, then stopped. 'You are sure?'

'Very sure.'

'Oh *God*, I love you too!' he groaned, gathering her into his arms to bury his face in her throat. He trembled against her as he strained her to him. 'If you only knew how I have longed to hear to say you love me,' he kissed her again and again, until they were both breathless. 'I desired you very much on our honeymoon, you must know that,' he said dryly. 'But each time I loved you I inwardly pleaded with you to show me some sign of love, to show I gave you more than physical pleasure. I have loved you for so long, since I helped you to stand after your accident.'

'But the day after we were married you said that if I hadn't been an innocent you would have ended our marriage.'

He shuddered against her. 'I could never have done it. Never! You are everything I have ever wanted in a woman, everything I will ever need. But you did not like me very much to start with, would not let me get close to you, and so when the chance came for me to marry you I grasped at it with both hands.'

'You really *wanted* to marry me?' She played with the buttons on his shirt, touching the warm skin beneath.

'Desperately. And I used your closeness to your father to get what I wanted, to trap you into marriage with me, hoping you would come to love me later on. I already knew that you were not immune to me physically.'

Sophie blushed. 'You're a wonderful lover.'

'I know you enjoyed what we did together as much as I, but it was not enough. I have never been a patient man, and that weekend at your parents' home I knew I could not go on any longer, merely a pleasant physical experience for you. It demeaned my love for you. So I left. I have been here ever since just waiting for you to call.'

'And drinking yourself to death,' she added sternly. 'The place is a mess, and so were you.'

'I have been drunk most of the time, so the tidiness of the apartment has not mattered to me.'

'Couldn't you have had someone clean it for you?'

'You dismissed my cleaner,' he reminded.

She had done so because she had wanted to care for their home herself. 'You could have hired someone else.'

'I did not want anyone near me. Oh, Sophie,' he kissed her long and passionately, 'I have missed you so much, longed for you so desperately. I have not worked on anything but your painting since we parted. I could do no other work. Without you I am nothing.'

'Do you think Daddy might have his portrait of me now?' she teased.

His arms tightened about her. 'As long as I can keep you he may have a hundred portraits of you.'

'I love you so much, Luke,' she kissed his throat. 'I don't ever want to leave you again.'

'You will never be allowed to,' he said with his old arrogance. 'I want you, you know,' he groaned against her earlobe.

She did know, could feel his pulsating desire for her. 'But you haven't eaten yet.'

He grinned down at her. 'Now it is you who are being mundane! I think I have enough strength to make love to my wife.'

Sophie took his hand and led him over to the bedroom. 'If you haven't I could always make love to you.'

He chuckled behind her. 'What an excellent idea!'

The smile they shared was very intimate. 'I thought you might like that.' The bedroom door closed quietly behind them, the outside world soon forgotten.

Masquerade
Historical Romances

Intrigue excitement romance

THE EAGLE'S FATE
by Dinah Dean

When Napoleon invaded Russia, Nadya had to walk from Moscow with her possessions on her back. She expected pity from Captain Andrei Valyev, but he seemed to hate her — why, then, had he rescued her from a fate worse than death?

MAN WITH A FALCON
by Caroline Martin

Richenda rather welcomed the excitement when the Civil War came to the very gates of her home, Black Castle. But that was before she had encountered the Royalist leader, Sebastian, Lord Devenish!

Look out for these titles in your local paperback shop from
10th July 1981

Mills & Boon
Best Seller Romances

The very best of Mills & Boon Romances
brought back for those of you who missed
them when they were first published.

In July
we bring back the following four
great romantic titles.

FIRE AND ICE
by Janet Dailey

To fulfil the terms of her mother's will Alisa had to be married
before she was allowed to look after her young half-sister, and
Zachary Stuart was the only man prepared to marry her. But
Alisa's idea of marriage differed very much from that of her
new husband!

THE IMPOSSIBLE MARRIAGE
by Lilian Peake

Old Mrs. Dunlop thought it was a splendid idea to leave her
large house and a lot of money to her great-nephew Grant Gard
and her young friend Beverley Redmund — on condition that
within six months they got married. There was one snag: the
two people concerned just couldn't stand each other!

WIND RIVER
by Margaret Way

Perri had come here to Coorain, in the Dead Heart of
Australia, to work, not to teeter on the brink of disaster with a
man like the cattle baron Gray Faulkner. But how could she avoid
it?

THE GIRL AT GOLDENHAWK
by Violet Winspear

Jaine was used to taking back place to her glamorous cousin
Laraine, and as it seemed only natural to Laraine and her mother
that Jaine should take on the difficult task of explaining to her
cousin's wealthy suitor that she had changed her mind about the
marriage, Jaine nerved herself to meet the arrogant Duque Pedro
de Ros Zanto. But there was a surprise in store . . .

If you have difficulty in obtaining any of these books through
your local paperback retailer, write to:

Mills & Boon Reader Service
P.O. Box 236, Thornton Road, Croydon, Surrey, CR9 3RU.

The Mills & Boon Rose is the Rose of Romance

Every month there are ten new titles to choose from — ten new
stories about people falling in love, people you want to read
about, people in exciting, far-away places. Choose Mills & Boon.
It's your way of relaxing:

July's titles are:

SUMMER FIRE *by Sally Wentworth*
Why had Pandora ensured that the haughty but charming Sir
James Arbory would never look at her twice?

CASTLES OF SAND *by Anne Mather*
Little Hussein was Ashley's son, but she must never let him know
who she was. How could she put up with the hostility of
Hussein's formidable uncle Alain . . .

SPITFIRE *by Lindsay Armstrong*
Rod Simpson had bought Bobbie's home and let her stay there.
But what happened when his sister got married and went away?

STRANGERS INTO LOVERS *by Lilian Peake*
There was nothing between Gillian Taylor and Randall West
any more, except two people, one who loved Gillian and another
who loved Randall. And of course, Gary . . .

ABDUCTION *by Charlotte Lamb*
The worst thing that had happened to Marisa was for her baby
to be snatched. It also brought her estranged husband Gabriel
back on the scene . . .

ONE OF THE BOYS *by Janet Dailey*
Petra Wallis fell in love with her boss, the dominating Dane
Kingston. But he had no more use for her as a woman than as
a technician . . .

THE FLAME OF DESIRE *by Carole Mortimer*
Sophie's marriage to Luke Vittorio was a mockery. She had the
best of reasons for knowing he was still having an affair with
her stepmother . . .

THE SAVAGE TOUCH *by Helen Bianchin*
Lee was very much attracted to Marc Leone. But nothing was
going to deflect her from her real goal in life: to marry a
millionaire!

MIXED FEELINGS *by Kerry Allyne*
Kylie's boss, Grant Brandon, was old enough to be her father.
So there was no need for his disagreeable nephew, Race Brandon,
to be so scathing about her!

A TASTE OF PARADISE *by Margaret Mayo*
Her fiancé had not told Cathy about the unyielding Grant Howard,
who lived on the island she had received as a wedding present . . .

If you have difficulty in obtaining any of these books from your
local paperback retailer, write to:

Mills & Boon Reader Service
P.O. Box 236, Thornton Road, Croydon, Surrey, CR9 3RU.